GUMMITCH

AND

FRIENDS

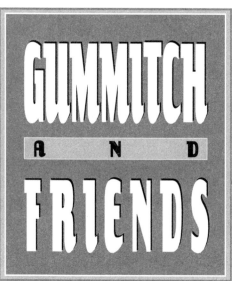

GUMMITCH AND FRIENDS

To Heather
— who also appreciates
Fritz Leiber and cats
— Poul Anderson

ILLUSTRATED BY
RODGER GERBERDING

FRITZ
AND FRIENDS
LEIBER

GUMMITCH AND FRIENDS

ACKNOWLEDGEMENTS

"Space-time for Springers" originally appeared in *Star Science Fiction Stories
4,* Copyright © 1958 by Fritz Leiber, renewed © 1986; "Kreativity for Kats"
originally appeared in *Galaxy,* April 1961, Copyright © 1961 by Fritz
Leiber, renewed © 1989; "Cat's Cradle" originally appeared in *The Book of
Fritz Leiber* Copyright © 1974 by Fritz Leiber, "The Cat Hotel" originally
appeared in *The Magazine of Fantasy and Science Fiction* October 1983,
Copyright © 1983 by Fritz Leiber; "Thrice the Brinded Cat" Copyright ©
1992 by Fritz Leiber; "The Lotus Eaters" originally appeared in *The
Magazine of Fantasy and Science Fiction* October 1972, Copyright © 1972 by
Fritz Leiber; "Cat Three" originally appeared in *The Magazine of Fantasy
and Science Fiction* October 1973, Copyright © 1973 by Fritz Leiber; "The
Bump" originally appeared in *Infinity 4,* Copyright © 1972 by Fritz Leiber;
"The Great San Francisco Glacier" originally appeared in *Booklet,* 7th
World Fantasy Convention, Copyright © 1981 by Fritz Leiber; "Ship of
Shadows" originally appeared in *The Magazine of Fantasy and Science Fiction*
July 1969, Copyright © 1969 by Fritz Leiber; "Earthbound," "God and the
Cat," "A Sinister of Siamese," and "Lullaby for a Cat" originally appeared
in *As Green As Emeraude,* Copyright © 1990 by Margo Skinner; "Origin of
the Species" originally appeared in *The Magazine of Fantasy and Science
Fiction* June 1958, Copyright © 1958 The Mercury Press, renewed © 1986
by Karen Anderson; "Sestina of the Cat in the Doorway" originally
appeared in *Smorgasbord,* Copyright © 1959 by Poul Anderson renewed ©
1987;
  Afterword Copyright © 1992 by Margo Skinner Leiber
  Introduction Copyright © 1992 by Fritz Leiber

Book design by Thomas Canty and Robert K. Wiener

Printed in the United States of America

ISBN - 1-880418-17-7 Deluxe Edition
ISBN - 1-880418-18-5 Trade Edition

FIRST EDITION

DONALD M. GRANT, PUBLISHER, INC.
HAMPTON FALLS, NEW HAMPSHIRE 03844

DEDICATION

for Margo

CONTENTS

ILLUSTRATIONS

INTRODUCTION

FRITZ LEIBER

INTRODUCTION

My first association with pet animals was with a dog instead of with any cat, an excitable little fox terrier named Paddy, provided for me by my parents on the traditional principle that a boy ought to have a dog. I was boarding for the public school year in Chicago with two aunts and an uncle-in-law while my father and mother toured in Robert Mantell's Shakespearian company. I envied them acutely.

The relationship between me and Paddy was formal and somewhat distant. It was an odd association: a melancholy and rather silent child and a nervous, darting, sharp-faced small dog. When the phone rang, or the door bell, he would bark excitedly, run in a circle, and likely nip whoever was near on the ankle. I recall suiting up after school and walking him up and down in front of our apartment building, for him to "do his business."

Later on, my parents and I got given a kitten in the summer place that my father built in Atlantic Highlands, New Jersey. This was more to my taste. I enjoyed seeing Nefertiti feed. She was handsome, and wonderfully silent. My imagination worked better around her.

Then after I went to college at the University of Chicago and got married, while we were on our honeymoon drive to meet my parents in Beverly Hills, California, Jonquil and I acquired two kittens, Murphet and Greyface. They were close bedroom companions who we watched closely and wondered at. We smuggled them into the ultra-modern hotel at San Antonio. These were the kittens to whom Lovecraft inscribed his gift of "The Cats of Ulthar" when we had our brief but

IX

intensive mind-bending friendship with him. They were certainly the first cats for which I felt a deep, though fumbling, sense of responsibility.

California was not good, in the long run, for either of them. Greyface died at the vet's of pandemic feline enteritis, the great cat killer at that time. Murphet was struck down by a speeding car outside our home in Beverly Hills. I remember going down in the night and finding him run over in the street. He seemed in such pain that I yielded to impulse and finished him off by beating his skull in with a brick. Next morning my father discovered him in the garbage and gave him a decent back-yard burial. My own tormented thoughts hadn't got that far.

Some ten years later, my wife, Jonquil, discovered and rescued Gummitch exactly as described in "Space-time for Springers." I took on myself the job of feeding him milk laced with vitamins, and given by eyedropper. The major incidents in this story, and in "Kreativity for Kats," were all enacted by him just as described—the business of the Squirrel Mirror, etc.—minus, of course, the incidents of the malevolent little sister and the attack on the baby. I remember I thought of him as co-author and paid him in tenderloin.

Jonquil and I were still managing most of his doctoring —the vitamins and the milk were our own idea—but when we moved from Chicago to California we remembered Greyface and had Gummitch innoculated against feline dysentery. He died some years later, at my mother's home in Pacific Palisades. He was never neutered. When we rescued another cat (Psycho in "Cat's Cradle") we had learned that this was a rational precaution to take, and had it done immediately.

By this time, cats had become regular features in several of my stories, and I had created the cat-lady, Tigerishka, in my novel, *The Wanderer*, so I brought her in as a leading character in "Cat's Cradle." Also, my novel *The Green Millennium* was originally called *The Green Cat.* Much later on, in 1983, I revived both Gummitch and Psycho for the story "The Cat Hotel," and still later, I wrote "Thrice the Brinded Cat" for this volume.

Over the intervening years, I've written several other cat stories, some of which, especially "The Lotus Eaters," have strong biographical elements. Now, looking back, I think I can safely say that as a result of my sympathic association with cats, the boy who puzzled over Paddy has become a somewhat more civilized inhabitant of planet Earth. I think I had this in mind when the semi-literate feline Kim acts as a hero's guide in the novella "Ship of Shadows," which I reprint in this volume for that reason.

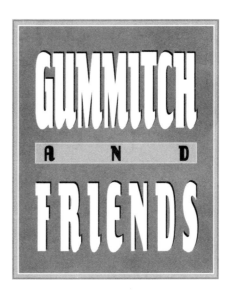

GUMMITCH AND FRIENDS

C O N T R I B U T O R S

MARGO SKINNER
KAREN ANDERSON
POUL ANDERSON

SPACE TIME FOR SPRINGERS

GUMMITCH:
OLD HORSEMEAT KITTY·COME·HERE.

Gummitch was a superkitten as he knew very well, with an I.Q. of about 160. Of course, he didn't talk. But everybody knows that I.Q. tests based on language ability are very one-sided. Besides, he would talk as soon as they started setting a place for him at table and pouring him coffee. Ashurbanipal and Cleopatra ate horsemeat from pans on the floor and they didn't talk. Sissy sat at table but they didn't pour her coffee and she didn't talk—not one word. Father and Mother (whom Gummitch had nicknamed Old Horsemeat and Kitty-Come-Here) sat at table and poured each other coffee and they *did* talk. Q.E.D.

Meanwhile, he would get by very well on thought projection and intuitive understanding of all human speech—not even to mention cat patois, which almost any civilized animal could play by ear. The dramatic monologues and Socratic dialogues, the quiz and panel-show appearances, the felidological expedition to darkest Africa (where he would uncover the real truth behind lions and tigers), the exploration of the outer planets—all these could wait. The same went for the books for which he was ceaselessly accumulating material: *The Encyclopedia of Odors, Anthropofeline Psychology, Invisible Signs and Secret Wonders, Space-Time for Springers, Slit Eyes Look at Life,* et cetera. For the present it was enough to live existence to the hilt and soak up knowledge, missing no experience proper to his age level—to rush about with tail aflame.

So to all outward appearances Gummitch was just a vividly normal kitten, as shown by the succession of nicknames he bore along the magic path that led from blue-eyed infancy toward puberty: Little One, Squawker, Portly, Bumble (for purring not clumsiness), Old Starved-to-Death, Fierso, Loverboy (affection not sex), Spook and Catnik. Of these only the last perhaps requires further explanation: the Russians had just sent Muttnik up after Sputnik, so that when one evening Gummitch streaked three times across the firmament of the living room floor in the same direction, past the fixed stars of the humans and the comparatively slow-moving heavenly bodies of the two older cats, and Kitty-Come-Here quoted the line from Keats:

> Then felt I like some watcher of the skies
> When a new planet swims into his ken;

it was inevitable that Old Horsemeat would say, 'Ah—Catnik!'

The new name lasted all of three days, to be replaced by Gummitch, which showed signs of becoming permanent.

The little cat was on the verge of truly growing up, at least so Gummitch overheard Old Horsemeat comment to Kitty-Come-Here. A few short weeks, Old Horsemeat said, and Gummitch's fiery flesh would harden, his slim neck thicken, the electricity vanish from everything but his fur, and all his delightful kittenish qualities rapidly give way to the earthbound singlemindedness of a tom. They'd be lucky, Old Horsemeat concluded, if he didn't turn completely surly like Ashurbanipal.

Gummitch listened to these predictions with gay unconcern and with secret amusement from his vantage point of superior knowledge, in the same spirit that he accepted so many phases of his outwardly conventional existence: the murderous sidelong looks he got from Ashurbanipal and Cleopatra as he devoured his own horsemeat from his own little tin pan, because they sometimes were given canned cat-food but he never; the stark idiocy of Baby, who didn't know the difference between a live cat and a stuffed teddy bear and who tried to cover up his ignorance by making goo-goo noises and poking indiscriminately at all eyes; the far more serious—because cleverly hidden—maliciousness of Sissy, who had to be watched out for warily—especially when you were alone—and whose retarded—even warped—development, Gummitch knew, was Old Horsemeat and Kitty-Come-Here's deepest, most secret, worry (more of Sissy and her evil ways soon); the limited intellect of Kitty-Come-Here, who despite the amounts of coffee she drank was quite as featherbrained as kittens are supposed to be and who firmly believed, for example, that kittens operated in the same space-time as other beings—that to get from *here* to *there* they had to cross the space *between*—and similar fallacies; the mental stodginess of even Old Horsemeat, who although he understood quite a bit of the secret doctrine and talked intelligently to Gummitch when they were alone, nevertheless suffered from the limitations of his status—a rather nice old god but a maddeningly slow-witted one.

But Gummitch could easily forgive all this massed inadequacy and downright brutishness in his felino-human household, because he was aware that he alone knew the real truth about himself and about other kittens and babies as well, the truth which was hidden from weaker minds, the truth that was as intrinsically incredible as the germ theory of disease or the origin of the whole great universe in the explosion of a single atom.

As a baby kitten Gummitch had believed that Old Horsemeat's two hands were hairless kittens permanently attached to the ends of Old Horsemeat's arms but having an independent life of their own. How he had hated and loved

25

those two five-legged sallow monsters, his first playmates, comforters and battle-opponents!

Well, even that fantastic discarded notion was but a trifling fancy compared to the real truth about himself!

The forehead of Zeus split open to give birth to Minerva. Gummitch had been born from the waist-fold of a dirty old terrycloth bathrobe, Old Horsemeat's basic garment. The kitten was intuitively certain of it and had proved it to himself as well as any Descartes or Aristotle. In a kitten-size tuck of that ancient bathrobe the atoms of his body had gathered and quickened into life. His earliest memories were of snoozing wrapped in terrycloth, warmed by Old Horsemeat's heat. Old Horsemeat and Kitty-Come-Here were his true parents. The other theory of his origin, the one he heard Old Horsemeat and Kitty-Come-Here recount from time to time—that he had been the only surviving kitten of a litter abandoned next door, that he had had the shakes from vitamin deficiency and lost the tip of his tail and the hair on his paws and had to be nursed back to life and health with warm yellowish milk-and-vitamins fed from an eyedropper—that other theory was just one of those rationalizations with which mysterious nature cloaks the birth of heroes, perhaps wisely veiling the truth from minds unable to bear it, a rationalization as false as Kitty-Come-Here and Old Horsemeat's touching belief that Sissy and Baby were their children rather than the cubs of Ashurbanipal and Cleopatra.

The day that Gummitch had discovered by pure intuition the secret of his birth he had been filled with a wild instant excitement. He had only kept it from tearing him to pieces by rushing out to the kitchen and striking and devouring a fried scallop, torturing it fiendishly first for twenty minutes.

And the secret of his birth was only the beginning. His intellectual faculties aroused, Gummitch had two days later intuited a further and greater secret: since he was the child of humans he would, upon reaching this maturation date of which Old Horsemeat had spoken, turn not into a sullen tom but into a godlike human youth with reddish golden hair the color of his present fur. He would be poured coffee; and he would instantly be able to talk, probably in all languages. While Sissy (how clear it was now!) would at approximately the same time shrink and fur out into a sharp-clawed and vicious she-cat dark as her hair, sex and self-love her only concerns, fit harem-mate for Cleopatra, concubine to Ashurbanipal.

Exactly the same was true, Gummitch realized at once, for all kittens and babies, all humans and cats, wherever they might dwell. Metamorphosis was as much a part of the fabric of their lives as it was of the insects'. It was also the basic fact underlying all legends of werewolves, vampires and witches' familiars.

If you just rid your mind of preconceived notions, Gummitch told himself, it was all very logical. Babies were stupid, fumbling, vindictive creatures without reason or speech. What more natural than that they should grow up into mute, sullen, selfish beasts bent only on rapine and reproduction? While kittens were quick, sensitive, subtle, supremely alive. What other destiny were they possibly fitted for except to become the deft, word-speaking, book-writing, music-making, meat-getting-and-dispensing masters of the world? To dwell on the physical differences, to point out that kittens and men, babies and cats, are rather unlike in appearance and size, would be to miss the forest for the trees—very much as if an entomologist should proclaim metamorphosis a myth because his microscope failed to discover the wings of a butterfly in a caterpillar's slime or a golden beetle in a grub.

27

Nevertheless it was such a mind-staggering truth, Gummitch realized at the same time, that it was easy to understand why humans, cats, babies and perhaps most kittens were quite unaware of it. How safely to explain to a butterfly that he was once a hairy crawler, or to a dull larva that he will one day be a walking jewel? No, in such situations the delicate minds of man- and feline-kind are guarded by a merciful mass amnesia, such as Velikovsky has explained prevents us from recalling that in historical times the Earth was catastrophically bumped by the planet Venus operating in the manner of a comet before settling down (with a cosmic sigh of relief, surely!) into its present orbit.

This conclusion was confirmed when Gummitch in the first fever of illumination tried to communicate his great insight to others. He told it in cat patois, as well as that limited jargon permitted, to Ashurbanipal and Cleopatra and even, on the off chance, to Sissy and Baby. They showed no interest whatever, except that Sissy took advantage of his unguarded preoccupation to stab him with a fork.

Later, alone with Old Horsemeat, he projected the great new thoughts, staring with solemn yellow eyes at the old god, but the latter grew markedly nervous and even showed signs of real fear, so Gummitch desisted. ('You'd have sworn he was trying to put across something as deep as the Einstein theory of the doctrine of original sin,' Old Horsemeat later told Kitty-Come-Here.)

But Gummitch was a man now in all but form, the kitten reminded himself after these failures, and it was part of his destiny to shoulder secrets alone when necessary. He wondered if the general amnesia would affect him when he metamorphosed. There was no sure answer to this question, but he hoped not—and sometimes felt that there was reason for his hopes. Perhaps he would be the first true kitten-man, speaking from a wisdom that had no locked doors in it.

Once he was tempted to speed up the process by the use of drugs. Left alone in the kitchen, he sprang onto the table and started to lap up the black puddle in the bottom of Old Horsemeat's coffee cup. It tasted foul and poisonous and he withdrew with a little snarl, frightened as well as revolted. The dark beverage would not work its tongue-loosening magic, he realized, except at the proper time and with the proper ceremonies. Incantations might be necessary as well. Certainly unlawful tasting was highly dangerous.

The futility of expecting coffee to work any wonders by itself was further demonstrated to Gummitch when Kitty-Come-Here, wordlessly badgered by Sissy, gave a few spoonfuls to the little girl, liberally lacing it first with milk and sugar. Of course Gummitch knew by now that Sissy was destined shortly to turn into a cat and that no amount of coffee would ever make her talk, but it was nevertheless instructive to see how she spat out the first mouthful, drooling alot of saliva after it, and dashed the cup and its contents at the chest of Kitty-Come-Here.

Gummitch continued to feel a great deal of sympathy for his parents in their worries about Sissy and he longed for the day when he would metamorphose and be able as an acknowledged man-child truly to console them. It was heart-breaking to see how they each tried to coax the little girl to talk, always attempting it while the other was absent, how they seized on each accidentally wordlike note in the few sounds she uttered and repeated it back to her hopefully, how they were more and more possessed by fears not so much of her retarded (they thought) development as of her increasingly obvious maliciousness, which was directed chiefly at Baby . . . though the two cats and Gummitch bore their share. Once she

29

had caught Baby alone in his crib and used the sharp corner of a block to dot Baby's large-domed lightly downed head with triangular red marks. Kitty-Come-Here had discovered her doing it, but the woman's first action had been to rub Baby's head to obliterate the marks so that Old Horsemeat wouldn't see them. That was the night Kitty-Come-Here hid the abnormal psychology books.

Gummitch understood very well that Kitty-Come-Here and Old Horsemeat, honestly believing themselves to be Sissy's parents, felt just as deeply about her as if they actually were and he did what little he could under the present circumstances to help them. He had recently come to feel a quite independent affection for Baby—the miserable little proto-cat was so completely stupid and defenseless—and so he unofficially constituted himself the creature's guardian, taking his naps behind the door of the nursery and dashing about noisily whenever Sissy showed up. In any case he realized that as a potentially adult member of a felino-human household he had his natural reponsibilities.

Accepting responsibilities was as much a part of a kitten's life, Gummitch told himself, as shouldering unsharable intuitions and secrets, the number of which continued to grow from day to day.

There was, for instance, the Affair of the Squirrel Mirror.

Gummitch had early solved the mystery of ordinary mirrors and of the creatures that appeared in them. A little observation and sniffing and one attempt to get behind the heavy wall-job in the living room had convinced him that mirror beings were insubstantial or at least hermetically sealed into their other world, probably creatures of pure spirit, harmless imitative ghosts—including the silent Gummitch Double

30

who touched paws with him so softly yet so coldly.

Just the same, Gummitch had let his imagination play with what would happen if one day, while looking into the mirror world, he should let loose his grip on his spirit and let it slip into the Gummitch Double while the other's spirit slipped into his body—if, in short, he should change places with the scentless ghost kitten. Being doomed to a life consisting wholly of imitation and completely lacking in opportunities to show initiative—except for the behind-the-scenes judgement and speed needed in rushing from one mirror to another to keep up with the real Gummitch—would be sickeningly dull, Gummitch decided, and he resolved to keep a tight hold on his spirit at all times in the vicinity of mirrors.

But that isn't telling about the Squirrel Mirror. One morning Gummitch was peering out the front bedroom window that overlooked the roof of the porch. Gummitch had already classified windows as semi-mirrors having two kinds of space on the other side: the mirror world and that harsh region filled with mysterious and dangerously organized-sounding noises called the outer world, into which grownup humans reluctantly ventured at intervals, donning special garments for the purpose and shouting loud farewells that were meant to be reassuring but achieved just the opposite effect. The coexistence of two kinds of space presented no paradox to the kitten who carried in his mind the 27-chapter outline of *Space-Time for Springers*—indeed, it constituted one of the minor themes of the book.

This morning the bedroom was dark and the outer world was dull and sunless, so the mirror world was unusually difficult to see. Gummitch was just lifting his face toward it, nose twitching, his front paws on the sill, when what should rear up on the other side, exactly in the space that the Gummitch Double normally occupied, but a dirty brown, nar-

31

row-visaged image with savagely low forehead, dark evil walleyes, and a huge jaw filled with shovel-like teeth.

Gummitch was enormously startled and hideously frightened. He felt his grip on his spirit go limp, and without volition he teleported himself three yards to the rear, making use of that faculty for cutting corners in space-time, traveling by space-warp in fact, which was one of his powers that Kitty-Come-Here refused to believe in and that even Old Horsemeat accepted only on faith.

Then, not losing a moment, he picked himself up by his furry seat, swung himself around, dashed downstairs at top speed, sprang to the top of the sofa, and stared for several seconds at the Gummitch Double in the wall-mirror—not relaxing a muscle strand until he was completely convinced that he was still himself and had not been transformed into the nasty brown apparition that had confronted him in the bedroom window.

'Now what do you suppose brought that on?' Old Horsemeat asked Kitty-Come-Here.

Later Gummitch learned that what he had seen had been a squirrel, a savage, nut-hunting being belonging wholly to the outer world (except for forays into attics) and not at all to the mirror one. Nevertheless he kept a vivid memory of his profound momentary conviction that the squirrel had taken the Gummitch Double's place and been about to take his own. He shuddered to think what would have happened if the squirrel had been actively interested in trading spirits with him. Apparently mirrors and mirror-situations, just as he had always feared, were highly conducive to spirit transfers. He filed the information away in the memory cabinet reserved for dangerous, exciting and possibly useful information, such as plans for climbing straight up glass (diamond-tipped claws!) and flying higher than the trees.

These days his thought cabinets were beginning to feel filled to bursting and he could hardly wait for the moment when the true rich taste of coffee, lawfully drunk, would permit him to speak.

He pictured the scene in detail: the family gathered in conclave at the kitchen table, Ashurbanipal and Cleopatra respectfully watching from floor level, himself sitting erect on chair with paws (or would they be hands?) lightly touching his cup of thin china, while Old Horsemeat poured the thin black steaming stream. He knew the Great Transformation must be close at hand.

At the same time he knew that the other critical situation in the household was worsening swiftly. Sissy, he realized now, was far older than Baby and should long ago have undergone her own somewhat less glamorous though equally necessary transformation (the first tin of raw horsemeat could hardly be as exciting as the first cup of coffee). Her time was long overdue. Gummitch found increasing horror in this mute vampirish being inhabiting the body of a rapidly growing girl, though inwardly equipped to be nothing but a most bloodthirsty she-cat. How dreadful to think of Old Horsemeat and Kitty-Come-Here having to care all their lives for such a monster! Gummitch told himself that if any opportunity for alleviating his parents' misery should ever present itself to him, he would not hesitate for an instant.

Then one night, when the sense of Change was so burstingly strong in him that he knew tomorrow must be the Day, but when the house was also exceptionally unquiet with boards creaking and snapping, taps adrip, and curtains mysteriously rustling at closed windows (so that it was clear that the many spirit worlds including the mirror one must be pressing very close), the opportunity came to Gummitch.

33

Kitty-Come-Here and Old Horsemeat had fallen into especially sound, drugged sleeps, the former with a bad cold, the latter with one unhappy highball too many (Gummitch knew he had been brooding about Sissy). Baby slept too, though with uneasy whimperings and joggings—moonlight shone full on his crib past a window shade which had whirringly rolled itself up without human or feline agency. Gummitch kept vigil under the crib, with eyes closed but with wildly excited mind pressing outward to every boundary of the house and even stretching here and there into the outerworld. On this night of all nights sleep was unthinkable.

Then suddenly he became aware of footsteps, footsteps so soft they must, he thought, be Cleopatra's.

No, softer than that, so soft they might be those of the Gummitch Double escaped from the mirror world at last and padding up toward him through the darkened halls. A ribbon of fur rose along his spine.

Then into the nursery Sissy came prowling. She looked slim as an Egyptian princess in her long thin yellow nightgown and as sure of herself, but the cat was very strong in her tonight, from the flat intent eyes to the dainty canine teeth slightly bared—one look at her now would have sent Kitty-Come-Here running for the telephone number she kept hidden, the telephone number of the special doctor—and Gummitch realized he was witnessing a monstrous suspension of natural law in that this being should be able to exist for a moment without growing fur and changing round pupils for slit eyes.

He retreated to the darkest corner of the room, suppressing a snarl.

Sissy approached the crib and leaned over Baby in the moonlight, keeping her shadow off him. For a while she gloated. Then she began softly to scratch his cheek with a long

34

hatpin she carried, keeping away from his eye, but just barely. Baby awoke and saw her and Baby didn't cry. Sissy continued to scratch, always a little more deeply. The moonlight glittered on the jeweled end of the pin.

Gummitch knew he faced a horror that could not be countered by running about or even spitting and screeching. Only magic could fight so obviously supernatural a manifestation. And this was also no time to think of consequences, no matter how clearly and bitterly etched they might appear to a mind intensely awake.

He sprang up onto the other side of the crib, not uttering a sound, and fixed his golden eyes on Sissy's in the moonlight. Then he moved forward straight at her evil face, stepping slowly, not swiftly, using his extraordinary knowledge of the properties of space *to walk straight through her hand and arm as they flailed the hatpin at him.* When his nose-tip finally paused a fraction of an inch from hers his eyes had not blinked once, and she could not look away. Then he un-hesitatingly flung his spirit into her like a fistful of flaming arrows and he worked the Mirror Magic.

Sissy's moonlit face, feline and terrified, was in a sense the last thing that Gummitch, the real Gummitch-kitten, ever saw in this world. For the next instant he felt himself enfolded by the foul black blinding cloud of Sissy's spirit, which his own had displaced. At the same time he heard the little girl scream, very loudly but even more distinctly, '*Mommy!*'

That cry might have brought Kitty-Come-Here out of her grave, let alone from sleep merely deep or drugged. Within seconds she was in the nursery, closely followed by Old Horsemeat, and she had caught up Sissy in her arms and the little girl was articulating the wonderful word again and again, and miraculously following it with the command—there could

35

be no doubt, Old Horsemeat heard it too—'Hold me tight!'

Then Baby finally dared to cry. The scratches on his cheek came to attention and Gummitch, as he had known must happen, was banished to the basement amid cries of horror and loathing chiefly from Kitty-Come-Here.

The little cat did not mind. No basement would be one-tenth as dark as Sissy's spirit that now enshrouded him for always, hiding all the file drawers and the labels on all the folders, blotting out forever even the imagining of the scene of first coffee-drinking and first speech.

In a last intuition, before the animal blackness closed in utterly, Gummitch realized that the spirit, alas, is not the same thing as the consciousness and that one may lose—sacrifice—the first and still be burdened with the second.

Old Horsemeat had seen the hatpin (and hid it quickly from Kitty-Come-Here) and so he knew that the situation was not what it seemed and that Gummich was at the very least being made into a sort of scapegoat. He was quite apologetic when he brought the tin pans of food to the basement during the period of the little cat's exile. It was a comfort to Gummitch, albeit a small one. Gummitch told himself, in his new black halting manner of thinking, that after all a cat's best friend is his man.

From that night Sissy never turned back in her development. Within two months she had made three years' progress in speaking. She became an outstandingly bright, light-footed, high-spirited little girl. Although she never told anyone this, the moonlit nursery and Gummitch's magnified face were her first memories. Everything before that was inky blackness. She was always very nice to Gummitch in a careful sort of way. She could never stand to play the game 'Owl Eyes.'

After a few weeks Kitty-Come-Here forgot her fears and Gummitch once again had the run of the house. But by then the transformation Old Horsemeat had always warned about had fully taken place. Gummitch was a kitten no longer but an almost burly tom. In him it took the psychological form not of sullenness or surliness but an extreme dignity. He seemed at times rather like an old pirate brooding on treasures he would never live to dig up, shores of adventure he would never reach. And sometimes when you looked into his yellow eyes you felt that he had in him all the materials for the book *Slit Eyes Look at Life* —three or four volumes at least—although he would never write it. And that was natural when you come to think of it, for as Gummitch knew very well, bitterly well indeed, his fate was to be the only kitten in the world that did not grow up to be a man.

KREATIVITY

F O R

KATS

Gummitch peered thoughtfully at the molten silver image of the sun in his little bowl of water on the floor inside the kitchen window. He knew from experience that it would make dark ghost suns swim in front of his eyes for a few moments, and that was mildly interesting. Then he slowly thrust his head out over the water, careful not to ruffle its surface by rough breathing, and stared down at the mirror cat—the Gummitch Double—staring up at him.

Gummitch had early discovered that water mirrors are very different from most glass mirrors. The scentless spirit world behind glass mirrors is an upright one sharing our gravity system, its floor a continuation of the floor in the so-called real world. But the world in a water mirror has reverse gravity. One looks down into it, but the spirit-doubles in it look *up* at one. In a way water mirrors are holes or pits in the world, leading down to a spirit infinity or ghostly nadir.

Gummitch had pondered as to whether, if he plunged into such a pit, he would be sustained by the spirit gravity or fall forever. (It may well be that speculations of this sort account for the caution about swimming characteristic of most cats.)

There was at least one exception to the general rule. The looking glass on Kitty-Come-Here's dressing table also opened into a spirit world of reverse gravity, as Gummitch had discovered when he happened to look into it during one of the regular visits he made to the dressing table top, to enjoy the delightful flowery and musky odors emanating from the fragile bottles assembled there.

41

But exceptions to general rules, as Gummitch knew well, are only doorways to further knowledge and finer classifications. The wind could not get into the spirit world below Kitty-Come-Here's looking glass, while one of the definitive characteristics of water mirrors is that movement can very easily enter the spirit world below them, rhythmically disturbing it throughout, producing the most surreal effects, and even reducing it to chaos. Such disturbances exist only in the spirit world and are in no way a mirroring of anything in the real world: Gummitch knew that his paw did not change when it flicked the surface of the water, although the image of his paw burst into a hundred flickering fragments. (Both cats and primitive men first deduced that the world in a water mirror is a spirit world because they saw that its inhabitants were easily blown apart by the wind and must therefore be highly tenuous, though capable of regeneration.)

Gummitch mildly enjoyed creating rhythmic disturbances in the spirit worlds below water mirrors. He wished there were some way to bring their excitement and weird beauty into the real world.

On this sunny day when our story begins, the spirit world below the water mirror in his drinking bowl was particularly vivid and bright. Gummitch stared for a while longer at the Gummitch Double and then thrust down his tongue to quench his thirst. Curling swiftly upward, it conveyed a splash of water into his mouth and also flicked a single drop of water into the air before his nose. The sun struck the drop and it flashed like a diamond. In fact, it seemed to Gummitch that for a moment he had juggled the sun on his tongue. He shook his head amazedly and touched the side of the bowl with his paw. The bowl was brimful and a few drops fell out; they also flashed like tiny suns as they fell. Gummitch had a fleeting vision, a momentary creative impulse, that was gone from his mind before he could seize it. He shook his head once more, backed away from the bowl, and then lay down with his head pillowed on his paws to contemplate the matter. The room darkened as the sun went under a cloud and the young golden dark-barred cat looked like a pool of sunlight left behind.

Kitty-Come-Here had watched the whole performance from the door to the dining room and that evening she commented on it to Old Horsemeat.

"He backed away from the water as if it were poison," she said. "They have been putting more chlorine in it lately, you know, and maybe he can taste the fluorides they put in for dental decay."

Old Horsemeat doubted that, but his wife went on, "I can't figure out where Gummitch does his drinking these days. There never seems to be any water gone from his bowl. And we haven't had any cut flowers. And none of the faucets drip."

"He probably does his drinking somewhere outside," Old Horsemeat guessed.

"But he doesn't go outside very often these days," Kitty-Come-Here countered. "Scarface and the Mad Eunuch, you know. Besides, it hasn't rained for weeks. It's certainly a mystery to me where he gets his liquids. Boiling gets the chlorine out of water, doesn't it? I think I'll try him on some tomorrow."

"Maybe he's depressed," Old Horsemeat suggested. "That often leads to secret drinking."

This baroque witticism hit fairly close to the truth. Gummitch *was* depressed—had been depressed ever since he had lost his kittenish dreams of turning into a man, achieving spaceflight, learning and publishing all the secrets of the fourth dimension, and similar marvels. The black cloud of disillusionment at realizing he could only be a cat had lightened somewhat, but he was still feeling dull and unfulfilled.

43

Gummitch was at that difficult age for he-cats, between First Puberty, when the cat achieves essential maleness, and Second Puberty, when he gets broad-chested, jowly and thick-ruffed, becoming a fully armed sexual competitor. In the ordinary course of things he would have been spending much of his time exploring the outer world, detail-mapping the immediate vicinity, spying on other cats, making cautious approaches to unescorted females and in all ways comporting himself like a fledgling male. But this was prevented by the two burly toms who lived in the houses next door and who, far more interested in murder than the pursuit of mates, had entered into partnership with the sole object of bushwacking Gummitch. Gummitch's household had nicknamed them Scarface and the Mad Eunuch, the latter being one of those males whom "fixing" turns, not placid, but homicidally maniacal. Compared to these seasoned heavyweights, Gummitch was a welterweight at most. Scarface and the Mad Eunuch lay in wait for him by turns just beyond the kitchen door, so that his forays into the outside world were largely reduced to dashes for some hiding hole, followed by long, boring but perilous sieges.

He often wished that Old Horsemeat's two older cats, Ashurbanipal and Cleopatra, had not gone to the country to live with Old Horsemeat's mother. They would have shown the evil bushwackers a thing or two!

Because of Scarface and the Mad Eunuch, Gummitch spent most of his time indoors. Since a cat is made for a half-and-half existence—half in the wild forest, half in the secure cave—he took to brooding quite morbidly. He thought over-much of ghost cats in the mirror world and of the Skeleton Cat who starved to death in a locked closet and similar grisly legends. He immersed himself in racial memories, not so much of Ancient Egypt where cats were prized as minions of the lovely cat-goddess Bast and ceremoniously mummified at the end of tranquil lives, as of the Middle Ages, when European mankind waged a genocidal war against felines as being the familiars of witches. (He thought briefly of turning Kitty-Come-Here into a witch, but his hypnotic staring and tentative ritualistic mewing only made her fidgety.) And he devoted more and more time to devising dark versions of the theory of transmigration, picturing cats as Silent Souls, Gagged People of Great Talent, and the like.

He had become too self-conscious to re-enter often the make-believe world of the kitten, yet his imagination remained as active as ever. It was a truly frustrating predicament.

More and more often and for longer periods he retired to meditate in a corrugated cardboard shoebox, open only at one end. The cramped quarters made it easier for him to think. Old Horsemeat called it the Cat Orgone Box after the famed Orgone Energy Accumulators of the late wildcat psychoanalyst Dr. Wilhelm Reich.

If only, Gummitch thought, he could devise some way of objectifying the intimations of beauty that flitted through his darkly clouded mind! Now, on the evening of the sunny day when he had backed away from his water bowl, he attacked the problem anew. He knew he had been fleetingly on the verge of a great idea, an idea involving water, light and movement. An idea he had unfortunately forgotten. He closed his eyes and twitched his nose. I must concentrate, he thought to himself, concentrate . . .

Next day Kitty-Come-Here remembered her idea about Gummitch's water. She boiled two cupfuls in a spotless enamelware saucepan, letting it cool for half an hour before using it to replace the seemingly offensive water in the young cat's

45

bowl. It was only then she noticed that the bowl had been upset.

She casually assumed that big-footed Old Horsemeat must have been responsible for the accident, or possibly one of the two children—darting Sissy or blundering Baby. She wiped the bowl and filled it with the water she had dechlorinated.

"Come here, Kitty, come here," she called to Gummitch, who had been watching her actions attentively from the dining room door. The young cat stayed where he was "Oh, well, if you want to be coy," she said, shrugging her shoulders.

There was a mystery about the spilled water. It had apparently disappeared entirely, though the day seemed hardly dry enough for total evaporation. Then she saw it standing in a puddle by the wall fully ten feet away from the bowl. She made a quick deduction and frowned a bit worriedly.

"I never realized the kitchen floor sloped *that* much," she told Old Horsemeat after dinner. "Maybe some beams need to be jacked up in the basement. I'd hate to think of collapsing into it while I cooked dinner."

"I'm sure this house finished all its settling thirty years ago," her husband assured her hurriedly. "That slope's always been there."

"Well, if you say so," Kitty-Come-Here allowed doubtfully.

Next day she found Gummitch's bowl upset again and the remains of the boiled water in a puddle across the room. As she mopped it up, she began to do some thinking without benefit of Concentration Box.

That Evening, after Old Horsemeat and Sissy had vehemently denied kicking into the water bowl or stepping on its edge, she voiced her conclusions. "I think *Gummitch* upsets it," she said. "He's rejecting it. It still doesn't taste right to him and he wants to show us."

"Maybe he only likes it after it's run across the floor and got seasoned with household dust and the corpses of germs," suggested Old Horsemeat, who believed most cats were bohemian types.

"I'll have you know I *scrub* that linoleum," Kitty-Come-Here asserted.

"Well, with detergent and scouring powder, then," Old Horsemeat amended resourcefully.

Kitty-Come-Here made a scornful noise. "I still want to know where he gets his liquids," she said. "He's been off milk for weeks, you know, and he only drinks a little broth when I give him that. Yet he doesn't seem dehydrated. It's a real mystery and —"

"Maybe he's built a still in the attic," Old Horsemeat interjected.

"— and I'm going to find the answer," Kitty-Come-Here concluded, ignoring the facetious interruption. "I'm going to find out *where* he gets the water he does drink and *why* he rejects the water I give him. This time I'm going to boil it and put in a pinch of salt. Just a pinch."

"You make animals sound more delicate about food and drink than humans," Old Horsemeat observed.

"They probably are," his wife countered. "For one thing they don't smoke, or drink Martinis. It's my firm belief that animals—cats, anyway—like good food just as much as we do. And the same sort of good food. They don't enjoy canned cat-food any more than we would, though they *can* eat it. Just as we could if we had to. I really don't think Gummitch would have such a passion for raw horsemeat except you started him on

47

it so early."

"He probably thinks of it as steak tartare," Old Horsemeat said.

Next day Kitty-Come-Here found her salted offering upset just as the two previous bowls had been.

Such were the beginnings of the Great Spilled Water Mystery that preoccupied the human members of the Gummitch household for weeks. Not every day, but frequently, and sometimes two and three times a day, Gummitch's little bowl was upset. No one ever saw the young cat do it. But it was generally accepted that he was responsible, though for a time Old Horsemeat had theories that he did not voice involving Sissy and Baby.

Kitty-Come-Here bought Gummitch a firm-footed rubber bowl for his water, though she hesitated over the purchase for some time, certain he would be able to taste the rubber. This bowl was found upset just like his regular china one and like the tin one she briefly revived from his kitten days.

All sorts of clues and possibly related circumstances were seized upon and dissected. For instance, after about a month of the mysterious spillings, Kitty-Come-Here announced, "I've been thinking back and as far as I can remember it never happens except on sunny days."

"Oh, Good Lord!" Old Horsemeat reacted.

Meanwhile Kitty-Come-Here continued to try to concoct a kind of water that would be palatable to Gummitch. As she continued without success, her formulas became more fantastic. She quit boiling it for the most part but added a pinch of sugar, a spoonful of beer, a few flakes of oregano, a green leaf, a violet, a drop of vanilla extract, a drop of iodine. . . .

"No wonder he rejects the stuff," Old Horsemeat was

tempted to say, but didn't.

Finally Kitty-Come-Here, inspired by the sight of a greenly glittering rack of it at the supermarket, purchased a half gallon of bottled water from a famous spring. She wondered why she hadn't thought of this step earlier—it certainly ought to take care of her haunting convictions about the unpalatableness of chlorine or fluorides. (She herself could distinctly taste the fluorides in the tap water, though she never mentioned this to Old Horsemeat.)

One other development during the Great Spilled Water Mystery was that Gummitch gradually emerged from depression and became quite gay. He took to dancing cat schottisches and gigues impromptu in the living room of an evening and so forgot his dignity as to battle joyously with the vacuum-cleaner dragon when Old Horsemeat used one of the smaller attachments to curry him; the young cat clutched the hairy round brush to his stomach and madly clawed it as it *whuffled* menacingly. Even the afternoon he came home with a shoulder gashed by the Mad Eunuch he seemed strangely light-hearted and debonair.

The Mystery was abruptly solved one sunny Sunday afternoon. Going into the bathroom in her stocking feet, Kitty-Come-Here saw Gummitch apparently trying to drown himself in the toilet. His hindquarters were on the seat but the rest of his body went down into the bowl. Coming closer, she saw that his forelegs were braced against the opposite side of the bowl, just above the water surface, while his head thrust down sharply between his shoulders. She could distinctly hear rhythmic lapping.

To tell the truth, Kitty-Come-Here was rather shocked. She had certain rather fixed ideas about the delicacy of cats. It speaks well for her progressive grounding that she did not shout at Gummitch but softly summoned her husband.

By the time Old Horsemeat arrived the young cat had refreshed himself and was coming out of his "well" with a sudden backward undulation. He passed them in the doorway with a single mew and upward look and then made off for the kitchen.

The blue and white room was bright with sunlight. Outside the sky was blue and the leaves were rustling in a stiff breeze. Gummitch looked back once, as if to make sure his human congeners had followed, mewed again, and then advanced briskly toward his little bowl with the air of one who proposes to reveal all mysteries at once.

Kitty-Come-Here had almost outdone herself. She had for the first time poured him the bottled water, and she had floated a few rose petals on the surface.

Gummitch regarded them carefully, sniffed at them, and then proceeded to fish them out one by one and shake them off his paw. Old Horsemeat repressed the urge to say, "I told you so."

When the water surface was completely free and winking in the sunlight, Gummitch curved one paw under the side of the bowl and jerked.

Half the water spilled out, gathered itself, and then began to flow across the floor in little rushes, a silver ribbon sparkling with sunlight that divided and subdivided and reunited as it followed the slope. Gummitch crouched to one side, watching it intensely, following its progress inch by inch and foot by foot, almost pouncing on the little temporary pools that formed, but not quite touching them. Twice he mewed faintly in excitement.

"He's *playing* with it," Old Horsemeat said incredulously.

"No," Kitty-Come-Here countered wide-eyed, "He's *creating* something. Silver mice. Water-snakes. Twinkling vines."

"Good Lord, you're right," Old Horsemeat agreed. "It's a new art form. Would you call it water painting? Or water sculpture? Somehow I think that's best. As if a sculptor made mobiles out of molten tin."

"It's gone so quickly, though," Kitty-Come-Here objected, a little sadly. "Art ought to last. Look, it's almost all flowed over to the wall now."

"Some of the best art forms are completely fugitive," Old Horsemeat argued. "What about improvisation in music and dancing? What about jam sessions and shadow figures on the wall? Gummitch can always do it again—in fact, he must have been doing it again and again this last month. It's never exactly the same, like waves or fires. But it's beautiful."

"I suppose so," Kitty-Come-Here said. Then coming to herself, she continued, "But I don't think it can be healthy for him to go drinking water out of the toilet. Really."

Old Horsemeat shrugged. He had an insight about the artistic temperament and the need to dig for inspiration into the smelly fundamentals of life, but it was difficult to express delicately.

Kitty-Come-Here sighed, as if bidding farewell to all her efforts with rose petals and crystalline bottled purity and vanilla extract and the soda water which had amazed Gummitch by faintly spitting and purring at him.

"Oh, well," she said, "I can scrub it out more often, I suppose."

Meanwhile, Gummitch had gone back to his bowl and, using both paws, overset it completely. Now, nose a-twitch, he once more pursued the silver streams alive with suns, refreshing his spirit with the sight of them. He was fretted by no problems about what he was doing. He had solved them all with one of his characteristically sharp distinctions: there was the *sacred* water, the sparklingly clear water to create with, and there was the water with character, the water to *drink*.

CAT'S
CRADLE

"But surely you of all people, Mr. Hunter, ought to believe in flying saucers," the Sexy New Neighbor said, gulping her brandy and keeping a long-eyelashed gimlet eye on the kitten Psycho, who had shown great interest in her wide-meshed pink net stockings. "Because for the last twenty-five years the saucer people have been telepathically giving all you science-fiction writers the ideas for all your stories, to prepare us humans for the day when they openly walk among us."

Old Horsemeat, known to human beings and other non-felines as Mr. Harry Hunter, muttered, "Or wriggle," and writhed his long frame a little and thrust forward his ill-shaven jaw and decanted some brandy into it, preparatory to further speech.

Kitty-Come-Here (Mrs. Helen Hunter to noncats), who had invited the New Neighbor over because Old Horsemeat was easiest to live with when he had a reasonable supply of sexy women around to lecture to on science and science-fiction and everything else, decided she had made an awful mistake.

Gummitch, surveying the scene with cool feline unconcern from his hair-hatched, black velvet cushion-throne in front of the fireplace, idly esped the hate-cat waves emanating from the Sexy New Neighbor and reminded himself to explain to Psycho soon that Legs, Especially Stockinged Female Ones, Are Not For Climbing.

Old Horsemeat splashed brandy in his own and the Sexy New Neighbor's goblets, frowned fiendishly, and said (while Kitty-Come-Here held her breath), "You know, Miss Neering, you are the first person—outside of Helen and, of course, the cats—to penetrate my secret. It's absolutely true that I regularly discuss science-fiction with a little old green man with a white beard who hails from

55

Arided. We do it almost every other night in the backyard at about three A.M. He gives me the office—the signal, that is—by tapping on our bedroom window with his third tentacle, the one that extends to twenty-seven feet. He passes me along some of the damnedest ideas. One was cat-burglary—that twenty-seven foot tentacle. Not stealing cats, of course (excuse me, Gummitch), but second-floor stuff like jewels and furs and black leather underwear. The old Aridedan's pretty kinky. His latest brain wave is how we could poison everybody not smart enough to drink and cook with sparkling water, by sprinkling a couple of ounces of plutonium hexafluoride in the city reservoir. His spaceship runs on P-hexy, so he's got lots of the stuff."

"He's testing your humanitarianism," the New Neighbor asserted confidently, sprawling her mini-skirted frame along the cat-scarred couch toward Old Horsemeat, though not with quite the enthusiasm and intense interest one might have expected. Most saucer addicts and even dabblers do not enjoy having the saucer scene stolen from them by squares—which includes all science-fiction writers, make no mistake.

"Yeah, I think you got it," Old Horsemeat agreed, absently dropping his hand to the New Neighbor's back and brushing it idly. It felt nice, but a little scaly. "That must be why he started putting up objections as soon as I said, 'Let's do it tonight.'"

"You were testing *his* humanitarianism," the sexy New Neighbor opined wisely, meanwhile luxuriating her shoulders, making what she thought were kitten noises, and taking a large sip of her brandy—no mean tally of simultaneous actions.

"Uh-uh," Old Horsemeat denied. "We got to solve the population explosion somehow. Which with skins like yours around is a toughie."

"We've always got the pill," she countered. "I'm speaking hypothetically."

"The pill'll never be an all-over answer," Old Horsemeat

replied darkly. "People get absentminded with boredom or excitement. Or they want buckets of kids to boost their egos or hold them together or get relief money. Or else they want to plain suffer for sex—the insufferable puritans."

Kitty-Come-Here sighed with relief, though keeping a watchful eye on exactly how far Old Horsemeat's idle brushing went. She took advantage of the interlude to snatch up Psycho exactly a quarter second before the kitten launched an all-out assault along the Sexy New Neighbor by way of the delectable long pink ratlines, which looked created to receive the tug of tiny claws.

Gummitch lowered his chin to his outstretched forelegs and regarded the scene with relaxed, utter boredom—which is a very beautiful expression so long as it is on the face of a mature cat.

Old Horsemeat got around to telling how the best thing about the little old green man was that he could do errorless final typing, a labor he performed in exchange for instruction in the art of writing science-fiction, so that he would be able to clean up when he got back to Arided, top star in the Northern Cross.

The Sexy New Neighbor knew when she was being had, or decided it was time to show she knew so, for she suddenly straightened up toward the end of the couch away from Old Horsemeat and gazing at the twisting puff of gray fur in the flexible cage of Helen Hunter's fingers, asked somewhat loadedly, "Why do you call him Psycho?"

"Her," Kitty-Come-Here corrected. "Yes, you can tell even at two months. She doesn't have the two little bumps. See? About the name, she actually was psycho at first, absolutely off her cat rocker. Gummitch led us to her. Some dear little children I'd enjoy tying up by their thumbs and lashing with a dog whip had shut her up for a day or so in a fuse box after petting her half to death. She was utterly kitten crackers the first two days after we rescued her, worse than a juvenile delinquent after a police storm. She'd hide in the television set and then scream, or purr and bite you. But then Harry hypnotized her with Gummitch's help and she snapped out of it and became almost too kitten-normal."

"What do you mean with Gummitch's help?" Old Horsemeat objected. "All by myself I shut off all the lights but one candle, and then I did the usual passes and strokings. You know." He had planned to demonstrate them on the Sexy New Neighbor, but then realized she was somewhat too big to be a convincing analogue of a kitten and, besides, she was now too far away to make the action seem unpremeditated.

"Soon as the kitten was in a light trance," he continued, "I told her about the Bill of Rights and how in this house it applies to cats even more than it does to talking, atom-bombmaking simians. Maybe that was a little over her head at the time—for instance, cats bear arms naturally and seldom have soldiers quartered on them—but I did convince her that, one, all children belong to an alien, utterly evil species, and that, two, decent relations based on full equality are possible between cat and man, no matter what goes on in furriers' and pounds."

The Sexy New Neighbor drew herself together around her brandy goblet. For when Old Horsemeat ended his ravings, Kitty-Come-Here merely nodded solemnly once and Gummitch turned on her a sinister gaze. She felt she had strayed into the old witch-house of a cat-centered Charles Addams family.

Psycho chose that moment to erupt from her finger-cage, flash like a gray streak past the Sexy New Neighbor, who dodged unnecessarily but quite understandably, and executed an almost incredible vertical leap, which ended with a soft landing on the mantelpiece, where she began coolly to wash herself.

"Did I remember to tell you cats can levitate?" Old Horsemeat demanded of the visitor. "Sure they can, all of them. But they hide it from us. They pretend it's just jumping. What a laugh! I think they all migrated here *circa* Four thousand B.C. from a high-gravity witch-planet. My old Aridedan's got a green cat thin as string beans that can jump over houses. Second- and third-story windows open even an inch are a cinch for him. He's kinky about women. He likes to crawl into bed with them, very softly. Then he slowly edges up to them under the sheets. His fur is silky as chinchilla. Then he bites them in the crotch."

The Sexy New Neighbor remembered she had to work tomorrow, gulped her nightcap, and somewhat dubiously accepted Old Horsemeat's offer to see her home next door.

She pointed at a sleeve-like arrangement in the bottom of the window next to the front door.

"What's that?" she asked.

"The cat door," Old Horsemeat told her. "You think this house is a prison?"

She concealed a shudder. Old Horsemeat didn't notice it and continued blithely, or did notice it and continued fiendishly as he swung open the human's door with a grandiose, loose-armed sweep and a bow. "Besides levitation and a lot of other secret powers, cats are the next brainiest animals to man—or maybe brainier and hide it—as is proven by their longevity. A cat can live twenty years, far and away the longest life-span for an animal anywhere near as small. And if you measure life-span by total lifetime heartbeats for a maximum-age animal, the cat comes at the top of the list after man—1,350,000,000 heartbeats, which is 150,000,000 more than the Methuselah of elephants. I'm sure that on most worlds the felines rather than the simians are the chief gnosiphoric family—that's a word I've just invented meaning wisdom-bearing. What's more, Miss Neering, or Eloise, if I may presume on an evening's conviviality . . ."

As he spoke, Old Horsemeat, reeling only a little, guided Miss Neering down the front steps, keeping a firm grip on her left upper arm while she kept an even firmer grip on the banister. Now as he steered her a weaving course across the lawns and as he shifted his subject matter from the felinocentric to the personal, his voice changed from oratorical to intimate and faded out.

Kitty-Come-Here overlooked the seeing-home operation from the front porch, where she had joined Gummitch for a breath of fresh late-summer air and a shower of moonlight. When Old Horsemeat returned, which was very soon, he walked in past them without a look or a word, poured himself a very large brandy, drank half of it down, and when the door had closed behind his cat and wife, exploded with, "God deliver me from that incredible kook! Not only a saucer nut, but she believes Bacon wrote Shakespeare—while riding in a saucer over New Atlantis, I suppose. It's the invariable sign of the crackpot—they believe not just some but all of the guff. Not only saucers and Bacon, but vegetarianism, reincarnation, compost farming, pyramidology, Hollow Earth, instant wisdom through psychedelic drugs, gut-level thinking smarter than Einstein's induced by bongo drums, the whole lot, besides being unalterably opposed to every chemical and engineering discovery that's holding our collapsing civilization together. Did you notice how she didn't turn a hair when I mentioned plutonium in the drinking water, but went pale when I added fluoride? What an ignorant bitch!"

And with that he snatched up Psycho, hurled himself back into the armchair beside which he'd just very carefully set his glass, and began to croon at the kitten, holding it to his chest and rocking a little, as if only that behavior could preserve his sanity. The kitten fought wildly for a moment, then quieted.

"Uh-huh," Kitty-Come-Here agreed with her husband, but without any great vehemence. She knew the habit husbands have of berating to their wives any woman to whom they are sexually attracted. She yawned. "I'm going to bed," she said, moving about turning out lights.

"Leave on that Tensor lamp across from me," Old Horsemeat said. "I've got to hypnotize Psycho first, and it'll do for a candle. That kooky woman got her all roiled up. My God, Helen, don't you realize it's cult-crazy people like her who are trying to kill science and hurry us into a new dark age?"

Kitty-Come-Here stopped, thought for a while, and then said judiciously, "I wouldn't worry about Miss Neering, Harry. I think her crackpot delusions are very superficial. Underneath she's much more interested in small, deep saucers of brandy than the flying kind, and in tall, sexy Earthmen rather than little old green men and kinky spider-cats from outer space." She started up the stairs.

Old Horsemeat shrugged. Rhythmically stroking Psycho, he began to croon in deep winning tones, "You're getting sleepy, little cat, very sleepy. You can hardly hold your head up. You're getting sleepier—"

Psycho started wriggling.

Kitty-Come-Here stopped on the sixth step and looked back at Old Horsemeat. "I am going to bed," she repeated. You can hypnotize Psycho all night. Or read Herman Hesse. Or get dead drunk and pass out on the floor. Nobody cares. This is Liberty Hall. But—" A new and somewhat knifelike tone came into her voice. "But— and I want you to listen to this, Gummitch—"

The big cat lifted his head from where he lay again on his throne and looked straight at Kitty-Come-Here.

"But," she continued, the word now a small explosion, "if that big brutal Svengali over there merely tries to stir out of this house tonight in the direction of Miss Neering's, say on the excuse of returning that kooky slut her compact and handkerchief—oh, we saw him shove them down in the crack of the couch, didn't we, Gummitch, when he thought neither of us would notice?—well, then you bite him, Gummitch, you bite him good and hard. And if he still persists, you come upstairs and bite me until I'm wide awake and insane with anger."

Gummitch dropped his head again with the effect of a curt

nod of affirmation. Old Horsemeat did not deign to reply. Kitty-Come-Here's footsteps proceeded upward and died out down the hall.

The living room was eerie with its one small cone of bright light in the great mass of semidarkness. Old Horsemeat chanted rumblingly, "You're getting sleepier and (yawn) sleepier, little cat. You can hardly hold your eyes open . . ."

Psycho began another bout of wriggling. Gummitch lifted his head again and eyed her with peculiar cat-to-kitten fierceness. Psycho quieted once more.

"You're getting still sleepier, little cat," Old Horsemeat rumbled on. "Every little cat muscle in you is relaxing (yawn) until you're limp as a dishrag. Now your eyes are completely closed. Your head is down. You're asleep, little cat, you're a . . ."

The hypnotism worked. Old Horsemeat's head sank back, his eyes closed fully, and his rumbling changed into a gentle snore.

Eyes bright as diamonds, Psycho held absolutely still in the big, limp hands.

For twenty seconds the comfortable, old living room was quiet as a crypt, except for the gentle snoring.

Psycho eased from between the hands, flowed down Old Horsemeat's trousered thigh, and landed beside Gummitch like a puff of coherent smoke.

Without a word or a look, Gummitch turned, made a short run past the Tensor's bright cone, and sprang through the cat door. Psycho swiftly followed, executing a comically frantic twist and a clawing pull midway.

They stood side by side at the top of the front porch steps. The faintly cool yet balmy night was alive (for cats) with many sounds, from the soft panting of a big dog in the high-fenced yard beyond Miss Neering's place to the stumbling walk of a nearby beetle over crisp, fallen leaves. Moonlight sprinkled down on them, a palpable silver rain. And there were cat-multitudinous sights (a many-layered world of sharp shadows) and scents and the pressure of a faint breeze on whiskers and fur, and the upward thrust of painted old wood under paw-pads.

Tonight this shadowy, silvery, murmury world was spiced with excitement and carried also a special call, yearning, imperious, and enravishing.

Gummitch made his head into a compass and slowly turned it this way and that, hunting the vector of the call. Finally a needle of nerves stopped rocking. His head and eyes were directed at the hedge in front of Miss Neering's place. Again without word or sidewise look, he trotted in that direction with Psycho loping close at his side, head level with the big cat's shoulder.

A fixed male cat, the Mad Eunuch, in whom neutering had produced a weird belligerence and with whom Gummitch had had many famous fights, came tracking after them as they reached the hedge and went slinking along it. But Gummitch paid the new and more careless paw-paddings no attention—even Psycho did no more than stiffen her silvery fur—and for once the Mad Eunuch did not run amok, only followed two dozen cat paces behind.

There also fell into line, still farther back, an almost skeletally gaunt alley cat, whom Old Horsemeat had nick-named the Flying Dutchman for his raggedy black, dirty-white, and reddish fur and his habit of approaching tremblingly and with infinite caution the Hunter back door and then tearing off in mad panic if someone came out or even if footsteps sounded too loudly inside. Gummitch himself had never been able to contact this unhappy hobo cat, for whom he felt considerable sympathy because of his own background as a starved and orphaned kitten. If he hadn't been rescued by Old Horsemeat and Kitty-Come-Here—and hadn't died—he might well have become such a dismal bindlestiff.

As the little cat cortege passed the hedge and started along the high fence beyond it, the big dog began to bark hysterically. But the cats ignored this utterly, except that Psycho jumped over

65

Gummitch, sudden as an electric shock, light and noiseless as a feather, and then proceeded along as if nothing had happened and as if her courage had never faltered, except that now she was on the bigger cat's larboard instead of starboard side.

Nor, across the street and moving in the same direction, did the big sleek black male and his silvery tiger consort take any note of the sudden torrent of canine noise.

Nor did even the Flying Dutchman do more than tremble a little harder as he single-footed forward. Evidently the dog found something eerie in this utter lack of reaction from cats to his most horrible threats, for his barking suddenly became more whimpering than hysterical and faded down abruptly as he fled to the protection of his porch and magic doormat.

Ahead was a small park with a grove of trees in its center, all balmy in the moonlight. It was there that Gummitch's compass led them—and not Gummitch's alone, for now it was clear that there was a trickling of cats from all the streets around—tabbies, Persians, Siamese, tiger and barred, alley, house, and store—and all silently and unconflictingly headed for the grove in the park.

A cop on his beat would surely have noticed them. But the two cruising by in their squad car could not see low-striding cats. In fact, they were becoming unable to see nighttime human pedestrians, except as potential rioters, thieves, looters, delinquents, and cop-killers.

An old drunk crouching away almost cat-low from the police headlights did notice the streaming cats and he studied them blinkingly, long after the police car was gone. Muzzily the thought came to him that a world with sights as strange as this might still be worth living in—or perhaps it was only that the delay lowered the alcohol content of his blood—at any rate, the hazy idea of suicide sank back down into his subconscious, like miasma into a marsh, and he turned back toward Skid Row from the street that led toward the river.

A girl saw the cats, though her boyfriend didn't. He was intent only on her. Arms around each other, they were headed toward the grove.

She thought the cats were kind of beautiful, but they spooked her.

So she said, "Honey, I've changed my mind. Like let's go to my place like we planned."

He said, "But, honey, you just said you were afraid your folks—"

She said, "I just remembered they're sure to be away all night. They *always* get stoned and pass out when they go to the Wilsons'."

He said, "I don't know, honey, it doesn't sound too safe to me."

She said, "Are you scared, honey?"

He said, "Of course not. But the way you keep changing your mind is driving me out of my gourd."

She said, "Please, honey, I'd *rather.* And it'll be *nicer.*"

He said fondly, "You're a freak, honey, a complete freak."

She said, "Besides, I'd get uptight with all these cats watching us."

He said, noting them belatedly, "Crazy. Must be Bast-worship night. Luna in Leo. Cats high and doing their God-thing. Make my nose run—not their fault, just allergy. OK, OK, honey. Anything you say."

As the lovers turned back, the cats flowed across the springy turf, their varicolored fur all bright platinum to gleaming obsidian in the moonlight, no spectral colors at all. As their first ranks entered the grove, there was a faint crackling of fallen leaves, and the platinum-obsidian became a moving variation of brightness in the moon-dapple everywhere.

No, not quite everywhere. Near the center of the grove, on the side away from the moon, was an ellipse of unbroken blackness a little more than twenty feet long.

This shadow was cast by a bulge-centered, flattish, circular object poised in the treetops exactly over the small glade in the middle of the grove. At first glance it would have seemed to rest on the branches all around. But then it would have been seen that the branches up there were hardly more than twigs, not strong enough to support such an object even if formed of thinnest aluminum. And in any case the twigs were not bent particularly downward. It would have become clear that the object, which resembled two huge saucers clapped together rim to rim, merely rested among the slim branches, held up by some invisible power of its own.

The cats filled the grove, crowding around the black ellipse, but none entering it, as if it were a black abyss and they all nosing at its brim.

A bough creaked and a large, slim shape dropped down to crouch effortlessly in a moon-pied, wide crotch midway between the circular vehicle and the ground. All the cats looked up, their eyes close-paired moonstones or pearls baroque with bulging, vertical black streaks.

"'Allo, li'l fren's," a soft yet vibrant voice called down. "I'm glad many of you came tonight, for I've news. May be a relief to some, and just may make a few sad for a while. But not to worry, any of you."

The accent of the voice was very strange and the tone stranger. If one can imagine the purring of a cat, or a tiger, shaped to human speech, shaped to English, one gets an approximation.

Stranger still perhaps, though most appropriate, all the cats below had begun to purr like sleepy beehives the instant the shape had dropped to the crotch.

"You 'ave a good week, li'l sneakers?" the voice continued in a note of affectionate badinage. "Meat, clear water, milk? The monkeys decent to you?"

The purring continued to rise like a low-pitched note,

sounded pianissimo, in an orchestra of cellos or viola da gambas. But here and there it changed to low wailings and mewings.

"Tha's bad. Tha's 'bominable. We'll kill us some nice people, eh? Kill us some hippies. Kill us some cops."

Gradually the shape became clearer in the moon-dapple. Imagine a figure midway between that of a leopard, a large cheetah, and a slender and supple young woman covered with short fur, and one gets an approximation. It crouched a little more like a young woman than a feline, but the hand by which it steadied itself had dark pads and long claws sharply curved at their tips. The feminity was definite. It was beautiful.

Suddenly it leaped forward out of moon-dapple into darkness and landed with hardly a sound in the center of the elliptical shadow. There it stretched prone, almost invisible except for the low silhouette it made with tufted ears and slowly switching tail, a slim recumbent sphinx. After a while there was the faintest glint of fur and claw and the glow of eyes whose pupils were like black flowers with five narrow petals tapering to points.

"Come on. Come to me," the voice purred. "Don' be scared."

There was a wait. Then Gummitch strode into the ellipse, his head high, his fur flat. Psycho moved anxiously and strained forward, but did not follow. The sphinx reached out a slim paw to catch Gummitch up, but instead of making his body yielding he stood with four legs straight and firmly planted, and she contented herself with softly tickling his chest and stroking his back, her claws retracted. He suppled himself without becoming limp and he twisted his neck appreciatively.

"I know you," she crooned, "you're the cool one. What is it you're called? Oh yes, of course, Goomitch—what a name! Trust the monkeys to think up one like that, bad as their language, which to tell the truth, Goomitch, I'd never have bothered to learn except I was bored and wanted to make familiar noises at you and your

69

fren's. Oh they're not all fren's eh? Well, it's the same with my people.

"But how about it, Goomitch, shall we get rid of the monkeys and put you cats in charge around here? Like it should be. Except you're all pretty little.

"What's that you say? There are big cats across the waters? Bigger even then me? Amazing!—I'll have to investigate if I still got the time.

"They're here too? In a big park? And you've seen them? Actually seen them yourself? Old Horsemeat took, no . . . *smoogled* you in under his coat? What kind of a monkey name is Old Horsemeat? Oh I see, it's your name for him, from what he feeds you.

"You tried to talk to the big cats, but they couldn't understand you? They were . . . stupid? That doesn't make sense. You know what, Goomitch, I don' think you and your fren's are related to them at all. I think you're all dwarf jester-cats and playcats lef' behind when some ship of my people made a landing here millennia ago. Your cats' cradle is in the stars, maybe. Anyhow, you should come to my planet! There you'd find all the cats as much smarter than you as you're smarter than mice.

"You don' think mice and rats are so stupid? Well . . . butterflies then, gol'fish.

"The big cats are dangerous? Now you're talking like a monkey. They keep them *behind bars? In cages? That's indecent! That's a crime against the universe!* The monkeys should be destroyed, if only for aest'etic reasons. I think I'll kill as many of them as I can before I go.

"You wouldn't like that? What kind of a cat are you, Goomitch? You've got a slave mentality! What do your fren's say?"

The slim sphinx lifted her magnificent head, tufted ears peaked, fur bristling, long whiskers a-twitch, lips drawn back from fangs, five-petaled eyes flashing.

70

The purring round about increased. The cats pushed closer inward, though still none of them besides Gummitch ventured from the moon-dappled space into the black ellipse. The circle of their small eyes gleamed like rosaries of pearls.

Slowly swiveling her head, the sphinx asked clearly, thrice, "Should I kill the monkeys?"

There were mewings, hissings, and wails, though the purring still predominated.

The black, five-pointed stars of the sphinx's pupils contracted and she looked upward a little and held very still, as if listening to the inaudible, and dissecting and numerating it.

At last she dropped her head and said, "Fft! They're slaves too, except for a few lonelies and blood-mads and some that, excuse my bad manners, aren't very right in their heads. I should have expected they were all cowards, when only one came when I called." Again she lifted her head. "Won' some more of you come to me, please? Won' jus' one?

"What's that, Goomitch? You're not a slave? You live with the monkeys as an equal? No, that can't be. Someone's—how do you say?—sold you a bill of goods.

"No, not even with one monkey is it possible. Monkeys are monkeys, always.

"I don' quite . . . Yes. Yes. Oh, now I understand. You think you control what your monkey does, or at least have fifty percent control? That's what every slave believes . . . when times are good. But when times are bad, when there's hunger, something stolen, something broken, a child scratched, then's the moment of truth. 'Allo, who's this?"

The sphinx's gaze went beyond Gummitch. Trembling in every emaciated member, and putting one shaking foot at a time in front of the next ahead, as if he were walking a tight wire, the Flying Dutchman had stepped across the boundary of darkness. His ears were laid back, his big-pupiled protuberant eyes stared, his ragged hair was irregularly erected, he panted, showing his yellow fangs, one of which was broken, and his slack, long, pale pink and black tongue lolled out the side of his mouth.

Finally he came within the sphinx's reach and stopped, as if he had expended all his courage and energy in the act of a lifetime. He swayed and almost fell over.

Far more slowly, tentatively, and gently than she had with Gummitch, the sphinx crept out a paw and touched him thistle-down lightly. As she feather-stroked him, he responded more swiftly and completely than Gummitch had and soon collapsed into the padded, fur-edged hand. She carefully lifted him and held him lightly against her breast.

"There, there, Flyin' Dushman," she crooned. "My, my, oh yes, but you've had a hard life. But you never been behind bars. You never los' your bravery." She looked up. "What's that you're askin', Goomitch? Oh, you noticed my 'if I still got the time' and 'before I go.' You got a mind like a detective. Well, it's true what you guessed. Listen to me, all of you! My subetheric SOS—after the explosion of the . . . *Sabertooth*, you'd say, with only me out-board—finally got noticed and a star-drive ship, bound from Alpha Libra 4 to the Pleiades, is picking me up at dawn at the top of your ionosphere about your South Pole."

The purring of almost all the cats turned to a subdued cater-wauling and to whimpering mews.

"Tha's nice," the sphinx said. "I'm glad you're sorry a lit-tle. I mus' say I'm a li'l sorry too, jus' on your account, though. I'll be glad to leave monkeyland!

"One thing more." With a final caress, she set the Flying Dutchman down as far away from her as Gummitch stood. The hobo cat reeled a little but then, although trembling once more, got his balance. "I 'ave space for three or four of you aboard. Who wants to come?"

The purring recommenced, became a great soft vibration.

All the cats in the moonlight strained forward one more time, yet not one entered the inky ellipse.

"'Ow about you, Goomitch?" the sphinx asked winningly. "You come with me, eh?"

From the edge of the ellipse, Psycho mewed anxiously.

Gummitch stared the sphinx straight in the eyes. Then without changing his gaze, he deliberately moved backward half the length of his body.

At the same time the Flying Dutchman gave a rasping, ragged "Phrrrt!" like an aged drunk trying to baby talk, and staggered forward. The sphinx caught him up again and said tenderly, laughing at herself, "So you's all I get, you old wreck, you ancient mariner. I bet you and your parasites burn out my demicrobing machine!"

Then she looked up. "Remember me," she said, impassive-faced. "Tell your kittens about me. Life's not so bad, here and now, you think. A few of you, like Goomitch, even dream of an impossible cat-man symbiosis. But the times will come again, even here, when you're hunted down as witch-things, yes, hunted for food. Remember me. And then when your day comes, as it will, put down the monkeys without mercy. And when you finally get the star-drive, come visit me at the Pleiades. Ask at any inhabited planet in the cluster. Remember."

When Kitty-Come-Here, clear-eyed, primped, and lace-robed, came briskly downstairs the next morning, Old Horsemeat was still asleep, pain-faced, with Psycho in his lap, while Gummitch was coiled on his cushion. As she went around to *whir* drapes apart and let in blasts of sunlight, the two cats wakened. Gummitch mewed a casual "Good morning," and started toward the kitchen. Psycho followed him.

Old Horsemeat's eyes slowly came ungummed. Then he gave a sizable start. "O my God, Helen," he said, "easy on that light. Why didn't you make me go upstairs to bed? I'm so stiff I know I'm going to break something unkinking."

"Up to bed?" she asked in mock amazement, whirring another set of drapes apart. "Why, I was letting you have your night on the tiles, and it's your own fault if you were too unenterprising to do anything but pass out and get creaky-jointed. For that matter I gave all three of you your night on the tiles, and none of you seems to have taken advantage. What stay-by-the-fires!"

"There wasn't any fire," Old Horsemeat complained morosely as he gingerly worked with his fingers at his neck and the small of his back. "In fact, it's still damn chilly, you would-be murderess."

Next door Eloise Neering woke with the thought, "That big, old, conceited lecher and his brunette Lucille-Ball wife! What a scene! And all those crazy cats!"

THE CAT HOTEL

From the cool patch of floor by the kitchen door Gummitch, an orange cat of endless curiousity and great patience, watched the younger and slenderer gray cat Psycho stand motionless over their water dish, peering down at her reflection. The day was hot, but she did not drink.

Although they were not related, Gummitch felt a big-brotherly concern for Psycho. He wondered if she were studying the mirror world or even considering oversetting the dish to create a water-sculpture as he'd done on occasion.

Or if something sinister were at work.

Kitty-Come-Here, their feather-brained mistress, known to humans as Helen Hunter, stopped in the dining room doorway, a small slender woman in a thin flowered dress carrying a furled green parasol and a small white handbag.

"I've called a taxi, Gummitch," she informed him, "to take me to the Concordia Convalescent Hospital to make polite inquiry of my beloved widowed mother-in-law as to how her broken hip is mending, and sweet worried noises. Though truly it is the great Harry Hunter's place to do that." She sniffed. "Don't you think, Gummitch, his business trips have come most conveniently since the catastrophe? I leave you in charge of the house. Please don't go out and pick a fight with the Mad Eunuch, it's much too sultry. Ah, there's the buzzer. Psycho, if you can stop admiring yourself for a moment and listen to me, be a good kitling and do everything that Gummitch tells you to, bar bedroom stuff. Now good-bye, chaps."

Gummitch himself rather wished that Old Horsemeat were here, not to pay dutiful filial visits, but to consult with about Psycho. Except that of late his strange parent-god had been imbibing rather too freely of the second of the two wondrous and terrible evil-tasting human beverages—not mind-quickening coffee, which had the power almost (but not quite, alas) to gift brutes with human speech, but insidious sometimes-burning alcohol, the mocker and jester—and as a result was not to be trusted as much as formerly.

Kitty-Come-Here, the ginger cat had to admit, was showing flashes of unaccustomed thoughtfulness and reliability—though not many or very bright, he hastened to add. Still and all, beneath her solemn kitteny playfulness, there did seem to be something new, serious and mysteriously sad, growing by fits and starts under the bobbed black hair of the little lady who had come to Old Horsemeat (to use his words) from over the Short-waved Ocean, in contradistinction to the Pacific.

The cat heard the front door close.

Somewhat later, at Concordia, Helen Hunter backed smiling and cooing out of Mrs. Hobart Hunter's single dim ground-floor room rather more hurriedly than she'd planned so as not, at all costs, to hear the deep sob she suddenly *knew* was going to burst convulsively from behind the bravely composed face and tightly pressed, serenely smiling lips of the cologne-scented old lady supine in the narrow high bed. For if she did hear it, she'd have to go back and do all her clucking, Harry-excusing work over again, and she as suddenly knew she simply couldn't *bear* that. Panic touched her, and in its unreasoning grip she backed rather faster and farther than she'd intended—all the way into the equally dim double room across the hall.

Gaining some control of herself, she turned around rapidly, surveyed the three beds and three old women crowding the room, and was momentarily shocked moveless and speechless, the contrast with what she had been visiting was so positively scaly.

Her mother-in-law had been tucked in neatly (of course she had a broken hip), while these creatures sprawled all which ways in their nightgowns (after all, it *was* warm) on top of their covers and pillows with all sorts of resultant untidy, immodest, even obscene disclosures.

In the single room there were a few neatly arranged objects on the bedside table and nothing whatever on the top sheet save Mrs. Hobart Hunter's pale flaccid arms extended decorously down her sides. Here all three beds and tabletops were littered with a jumble of soiled crumpled tissues, hair-holding combs and brushes, candy boxes, lunch remnants, paper cups, photographs, books, papers, and magazines, mostly astrology.

Harry's mother had been recently washed and neatly groomed, smelled of cologne.

These women had elf-locked or straggly flying hair, what there was of it, smeared lipstick, were smudged with dirt, looked greasy. They had a variety of odors about them. Really, they stank.

The first old woman had scrawny legs, a chunky pot-bellied body, and a little screwed-up face with squinting eyes and a button nose that would have looked scowly-angry except her small mouth was smiling.

The second old woman was fat like a little bumpy mountain with immense hips, droopy jowls, and large peering pop-eyes.

The third old woman was skinny as death itself, had a blotched pallor all over, a curving beak of a nose, and no chin to speak of. An empty brass cage hung beside her bed.

Helen took in all this in three rapid snapshots, as it were. A couple more seconds and she might have recovered her poise, but just then the first old woman asked with a chuckle, "lose your way, dearie?"

"Something frighten you, chickie?" the third old woman chimed like a cracked bell.

"Well, you certainly aren't my niece Andrea," the second old woman observed in a voice like suet.

"No, I don't believe I am," Helen started to say inanely and broke off midway, flustered.

"My, what a lovely green parasol," the third old woman continued.

"And what lovely bobbed hair. You do look cool," the first old woman added enviously.

"You look nice enough to eat," the second old lady concluded in her flannel tones.

"Oh, do please excuse me," Helen began and then turned and ran out before she garbled anything more or yielded to the impulse to respond to the last remark with "Is *that* what made you so fat, you dirty old cannibal?"

In her hurry she turned the wrong way in the hall, and rather than repass Mrs. Hobart Hunter's door and risk hearing snuffles, she left the Concordia by the way of the door to the concrete-surfaced "patio" surrounded on three sides by a tall hedge, which was simply the backyard of the one-story convalescent hospital and figured as an airing spot for the mostly elderly patients.

It was empty now, save for a few white tables and chairs in need of a paint job, and very hot. Helen unfurled her parasol and departed by the one exit available if you didn't want to go back through the Concordia, a two-foot gap in the back hedge—she had to tip her parasol to get through.

She emerged in an untidy, unpaved alley with garbage cans. From the newspapers scattered around them the words "Korea," "239 Communists," "McCarthy," and "Rosenbergs" leaped up, reminding her of how Harry had said to

Gummitch, "We live in a witch-hunt age, you hear me, cat? They got the diplomats and movie actors. They'll be after writers next, writers and cats. Remember how the Inquisition got after you along with the witches? Maybe the FBI will come for you and me at the same time."

Across the alley was another tall hedge with a matching gap in it, through which she could see a wedge of very green lawn that looked much more attractive than the littered sandy alley, so she pressed on through, tipping her parasol again and noting that the way underfoot was somewhat worn, as if these back exits were in regular use.

The gap was in a back corner of the property she entered. Straight ahead of her, the intensely green lawn stretched to the next street and was so thick and springy underfoot she was reminded of her native England.

There emerged into view a neat two-story wooden Victorian house whose gleaming white paint put the Concordia to shame. By its back door there was parked a shining white motor scooter with a white box fixed behind its sheepskin saddle. A narrow walk of pale gravel led from it close around the house to the next street.

Just next to Helen at the back of the property was a large area enclosed by a neat mesh-wire fence several feet higher than the hedge. Inside it were more lawn, three graceful low trees, some tidy bushes, two flower beds, and a low summer house (it looked) white as the main building with a white scrollwork sign over its open door that read, in much-serifed black letters, "Wicks Cat Hotel."

As she strolled wonderingly forward around the enclosure, Helen congratulated herself that her green parasol and flowered dress suited her very well to this handsome environment. Thank goodness, she told herself, she'd washed her hair and taken a shower just before coming out.

Coming around in front of the enclosure, where there was a latched door in the mesh, she surveyed it more closely, at once spotting a tranquil Himalayan on a tiny platform in one of the low trees and two strolling lilac-point Siamese slender as fashion models. The longer she looked, the more cats she saw ensconced in the bushes, sniffing the flowers, and wandering in and out of the little building, all of them elegant and well behaved, a few rather plain tabbies among the aristocracy, which included a blue Persian, a crinkly coated dark silver Rex, and a Havana brown who positively flamed. She said aloud softly, "Oh, Gummitch, if you could see this. A positive cat heaven!"

"Some persons do voice that reaction. But who is Gummitch, pray?"

Helen turned to face a trim woman her own age, two inches taller, fully as slender, but a degree sturdier than herself. A straw blonde, she wore her hair cropped and white slacks and Nehru jacket at once medical, military, and chic. Her right eye was deep blue, the other brown.

"He's my cat," Helen said eagerly, and when the other did not at once respond volunteered, "I'm Helen Hunter."

"Wendy Wicks," the other responded, extended her hand. "I'm the proprietor. Do I rightly discern in your speech a British accent with the lilt of Wales?"

Nodding, Helen countered, "And I a Scot's?"

"Truly enough, though I come from the Lakes. Which makes us fellow countrymen," the other said approvingly, adding an extra squeeze to their handshake. "Would you care to look inside?" She unlatched the mesh door. Helen furled her parasol.

The guests of the Wicks Hotel took no notice of them. Inside the low white building the two women stood comfortably enough, though Helen noted Harry would have had to stoop here. It was all one room lined with about sixty comfortably large cages in three tiers, each with its rug, water and food dish, and cat-box. The floor was occupied only by some hassocks, a climbing frame, and an imposing gray Tudor castle of stout cardboard with numerous cat-size windows and doors.

Helen echoed herself with, "A cat paradise!"

Wendy ended her little talk with, "Some of our guests are quite long-term, while their mistresses go to New York or London for the plays, or on extended ocean cruises," and gave Helen a hotel card on which her first name was spelled "Wendele," and had the initials "D.V.M." behind, and there was the subscript "hospital facilities available."

Wendy said, "The next time you're out of town, Gummitch might enjoy our hospitality. That is, unless he's an unneutered male."

"He is," Helen informed her. "My husband, Harry, has very fixed ideas upon that point—"

"I know," the other interposed with a touch of venom, "men are apt to entertain such barbarous notions."

"—and so do I, I was going to say," Helen concluded bravely.

Wendy caught her hand and squeezed it saying with a disarming smile, "There are, of course, my dear, good arguments, aside from patristic ones, to be made for that position. Even the Amazons had to make compromises. Why, I've taken toms myself in the hospital. Come, let me show you that."

Helen followed her out of the hotel and its grounds up to the back door of the Victorian house. As they passed the motor scooter Wendy touched it, saying, "Our ambulance," then, as she opened the white door beyond, "The Wicks Cat Hospital! No other species accepted!"

Inside was a spotless veterinary examination—and, Helen supposed, emergency room—everything cat-sized and

-adapted. Suspended on brass wires from points along the skull, spine, and tail was the complete skeleton of a cat, which struck her as rather grisly. A large 1953 calendar on the wall featured phases of the moon.

Wendy said, "Wait a minute and I'll show you our isolation ward for infectious cases. I'll call you," and she pushed through one of the two inner doors.

Helen peeked after her in time to see her draw a black curtain in front of three cages like those in the hotel, then drew back a little guiltily.

"Come in," Wendy called and when Helen had complied pointed out three glass-fronted large white boxes against the wall opposite the three curtained cages.

"Our isolation cubicles," she explained. "They have their own ventilation system."

Two of the boxes were empty. The other held a young seal-point Siamese, who peered out at them bright-eyed enough.

"I detected a mild respiratory infection in this one of our guests," Wendy explained, "and am treating it with antibiotics. She'll probably return to the hotel tomorrow." The phone in the examination room rang. "Excuse me," she said.

Alone, after a few seconds Helen yielded to curiosity. She crossed the room and started to lift a corner of the black curtain.

"Mrs. Hunter!" the other called from the doorway, "do you realize that cats are subject to certain diseases in which their eyes become temporarily hypersensitive to light? You might have permanently injured one of our patients."

"I'm sorry, I didn't know," Helen said, backing off.

"I think you had best leave," the other went on in a gruff doctor voice, and as she escorted a flurried Helen through the other inside door of the examination room through a long old-fashioned parlor with a large fireplace, continued formidably, "In the past, Mrs. Hunter, persons have gained entry to these premises under false pretenses with the intention of kidnapping valuable cats to hold for ransom and for even worse purposes!" Her mis-matched eyes flashed coldly.

"You surely don't think that I—" Helen began, more apologetic than indignant.

"No, I suppose not, I guess," Wendy replied with sudden and surprising return to her earlier amiability, "but after all, Helen, I have showed you everything here, and I'm sure that we both have other things to do." She led Helen into a front hall with a wide staircase leading to the second story. Then, as she let her out the front door, where a brass plate read "Wicks Cat Hospital," she gave Helen's hand a final squeeze and said with a smile, "Come back for another visit, dear, anytime you wish. Only remember that I'm another lone Britisher in an alien land and a profession dominated by arrogant males, so I have become overly sensitive and suspicious."

Hastening home by bus, Helen's feelings were mixed. She still felt drawn to Wendy. Such a strong, handsome, competent girl with a really beautiful face if you made allowance (if that were needed) for slightly over-large ears, though growing close to the skull, and of course the intriguing blue-brown eye pair. Why, it was years and years since she'd noticed so much about a person she'd met only once. Am I becoming infatuated? she asked herself with a silent giggle.

But then, on the other hand, the veterinary's sudden exaggerated hostility and the rather shivery details of the cat skeleton and black curtain. What had been behind that, anyway? The light-sensitive story was surely a blind because the light in the "isolation ward" had been on when the doctor'd first gone in and drawn the curtain.

And yet at the same time the whole place had reminded her so much and so nostalgically of England—the lawn, the house and cat motel, the woman herself—half-awakening deep-buried memories of all sorts, some of them, Helen felt sure, very strange.

When she left the bus, the day, though more sultry than ever, had darkened, and when she stuck her key in her own front door, she heard a low rumble of thunder.

Gummitch was waiting inside, uttering a "Mrrp-Mrrp!" in which there was more alarm and indignation than greeting. He ran halfway up the stairs and then paused to look back over his shoulder. Heart sinking, Helen followed him to the upstairs bathroom, where Psycho lay curled motionless in the pale green washbowl as though it was a cat sarcophagus. The young cat seemed only half-conscious; her eyes were filmed, her short gray fur was rough, her nose hot.

Helen carried her downstairs to the phone and dialed the number on the card given her by Wendy, who answered on the third ring, listened to Helen's rapid description, and said only, "Don't do anything, I'll be there."

Waiting would have been easier for Helen if she'd been told to do something. She opened the front door to the gathering dark and low growling thunder. She asked, "Whatever happened, Gummitch? Did Psycho go out and eat something? But the orangy cat answered only, "Mrrp-Mrrp!" Finally she called a taxi.

As if that had been the proper charm to hurry events, there was a purring "put-put" from down the street. Going to the door with Gummitch close beside her, she saw that the approaching storm had banished twilight and brought on instant night, into which the pale shape of the hospital scooter and rider came like the ghost of a modern centaur. It nosed into the driveway, then rode diagonally across the lawn to park at the foot of the front steps.

Wendy was now wearing additionally a white cap with rather long visor, and she stripped off white gauntlets as she came up the steps, carefully took Psycho into her arms, and briefly examined her.

"She's very sick and must be taken to the hospital at once and given treatment," she pronounced. "I'll have a full report for you tomorrow morning. Don't worry too much: she's a young cat and I believe we've caught it in time. Her chances of complete recovery are very good." All this while carrying Psycho down the steps, gently laying her in the box behind the saddle, which opened at a touch, and getting astride the vehicle, having thrust her gauntlets in the top of her slacks.

"Good-bye, chaps," she called as she drove off carefully at an even pace.

It all happened so fast that Helen, who'd hurried down the steps with Gummitch after her, couldn't think what to call back. But now as they both watched the white scooter disappear down the dark street, she said, "Oh, Gummitch, what have we done to Psycho?"

"Warra warra," the cat replied, concerned and somewhat angry. He hadn't liked the cat doctor's looks, and he also believed that his own close presence was in any case something essential to Psycho's safety and recovery.

Thunder rumbled, closer now.

A taxicab drew up. Its driver got out and, seeing Helen, opened the rear door and came a few steps up the walk.

She arrived at a quick decision, called to him, "I'll just get my bag and wrap; be with you in a second," and ran up the steps into the house, thinking Gummitch had run back ahead of her; cars often had that effect on him.

But the cat had other ideas. He'd circled off sideways

into the darkness, made a craftily wide circle through some bushes, and sneaked into the cab when the driver wasn't looking.

Inside he did not spring on the seat, but instead crouched in the dark far corner of the floor. He did not intend the investigations he had in mind to be thwarted. And indeed when Kitty-Come-Here got in, she was so busy giving the driver instructions as to where the Wicks Cat Hospital was, and so agitated generally, that she actually didn't notice him. She slung her light coat on the seat beside her, and it trailed over, further concealing him.

Gummitch congratulated himself on his sagacity. What doesn't move in the shadows, isn't seen. Old Horsemeat had more than once recited to him Eliot's poem about McCavity, the mystery cat modeled on Professor Moriarty, and if there were a Moriarty, there had to be a cat Sherlock Holmes, didn't there?

When the cab drew up at the newly repainted old white house with the brass plate beside the door and Kitty-Come-Here got out, saying to the driver, "Please wait for me," Gummitch slid out right behind her and immediately ducked under the vehicle, preparatory to beginning another of his wide circles. Geometric evasiveness, that's one more of my methods, he told himself.

Helen mounted to the open porch and pushed the buzzer, and when it wasn't answered quickly, plied the brass knocker, too. But when the door was finally opened, it was by an un-smiling and doctor-faced Wendy, who did not move aside to let her in.

"It's past visiting hours," she said coldly. "Really, Helen, I know you're concerned about your cat, but you mustn't become hysterical. You can't see Psycho now in any case; she's in isolation."

"But you didn't even tell me what's wrong with her," Helen protested.

"Very well. Your cat is suffering from epidemic feline enteritis, the most widespread and dangerous cat plague of them all, one for which early immunization is a necessary precaution observed by all half-way informed owners. But you never had shots for her, did you? No, I thought not. Perhaps your husband doesn't believe in that, either."

Gummitch watched the two from the next to the top step of the stairs to the porch, only his narrowed eyes showing over. When the cat doctor was in the midst of her condescending and reproachful lecture, he flowed up onto the porch and along it to the second window from the door, which was open wide at the bottom, and softly looped through, hugging the wall and sill, into the dim large room beyond.

Outside, the cat doctor continued, "What treatment is she getting? I injected serum and water in proper quantity, gave by mouth a chemical agent I've had good results with, and disposed her comfortably in an isolation cubicle, where she is getting *rest,* which is something even veterinary doctors require and get on rare occasions, and you no doubt could do with yourself. Please do not call before 9 a.m. tomorrow. Good night, dear Helen." And she closed the door.

After a moment of staring at it with both fists clenched, Helen returned to her cab, disconsolate and fuming delicately. The driver asked her, "Excuse me, lady, but did you have a cat with you in there when we came over?"

"Certainly not!" she replied impatiently. "Why do you ask?"

"I don't know," the driver responded warily. "I just thought . . ." His voice trailed off.

I shouldn't have been so short with him, she told herself. Natural of him to suppose that when you go to a cat hospital you take a cat. Probably thought I had it wrapped in my coat or something. Nevertheless, the matter worried her a little. Now she wouldn't feel easy until she'd seen Gummitch. But when she did, at least she could speak out her mind to him, relieve her injured feelings a little. Oh, that wicked (but so dashing) doctor woman!

In the Wicks Cat Hospital living room, Gummitch had immediately found a good hiding place under an easy chair against a wall, from which he could survey the whole room, study the black carpet with its curious designs in white lines, and wait until things settled down before beginning his detective work—see which way the cat doctor was going to jump, you might put it.

After shutting the door on Helen, she came rapidly through the living room (Gummitch saw only her trousered legs footed with white oxfords) and went through the swinging door at its back end. Outside, thunder crackled. The storm was definitely getting nearer.

After enough time for Gummitch to go into a half-doze, the cat doctor returned, setting the swinging door wide open, he was happy to see, though he could have managed it himself, he was confident, as well as many knobs and some latches.

She moved more thoughtfully this time, going to one of the bookcases and selecting a volume to take with her, before exiting to the front hall, leaving dimmed lights behind her everywhere. He heard her going upstairs.

Helen was in a quandary. She'd paid off the taxi driver, tipping him generously to make up for her shortness with him, but when she'd gone into the house there'd been no Gummitch to greet her and hear what she thought of the doctor woman. He might have gone out through the cat door, of course, on some business of his own, but wouldn't he have waited to ask her about Psycho? Had the taxi driver really seen a cat? Despite Wendy's warning she dialed again the number on the card, but this time got only an answering service which could just take messages to give the doctor when and if she called in. Outside, thunder boomed. Helen didn't like being all alone in the house.

Back in the living room of the cat hospital, the cat-detective still bided his time under the easy chair. After another period of waiting, during which there were faint footsteps overhead that finally ceased—the cat doctor's and some-one else's, still lighter but thumpy ones—Gummitch ventured out and unhurriedly made his way toward the back of the room, frequently pausing to sniff. Outside, the crackling came more often, and suddenly he heard the patter, then the pelting of swift-breaking rain, and from the window behind him felt a breath of chilly storm-breeze.

The white-line pattern on the black carpet was a curious one of triangles and triskelions and swastikas, and just in front of the cold, empty but practical fireplace and with one of its five points aimed straight at it, a huge empty star. There welled up in his mind a murky racial memory of an even wider hearth with a huge fire blazing in it and naked women standing before it in a pentacle and rubbing into each other's bodies an ointment that had a not altogether unpleasing acrid odor.

Gummitch glided into the examination room, saw the hanging cat skeleton, hissed under his breath, then sprang to the table before it, and gave it an experimental pat. The little bones rattled softly and the skull swung a bit, as if to see who its disturber was.

He next entered the isolation ward, the door of which was also set open. Perhaps because of the soft purr of their ventilation system, his gaze fixed at once on the three glass-fronted isolation cubicles, and he leaped lightly to the shelf in front of them.

In the cubicle Psycho lay on her side with eyes closed and ears drooped. He couldn't repress a mew of excitement, then, with his muzzle pressed against the glass, mewed softly twice more and rapped the pane lightly with a paw. She did not stir.

The young Siamese in the next cubicle was making motions at him, but Gummitch ignored her, continuing to study Psycho. He could discern her gray chest rise and fall a little, regularly, while her fur looked a little brighter than it had in the pale green washbowl, he thought—or hoped.

He reminded himself then that he was a detective in enemy territory and couldn't afford to give way for long to dumb dutifulness. With an effort he tore his gaze away from Psycho's window, turned to survey the rest of the isolation ward, and saw for the first time the three now uncurtained wire cages against the opposite wall.

The fur on his back rose and his tail thickened.

In the first cage was a little old dog with squinched-up face and beady eyes that glared at him continuously, a black Pekinese.

In the second cage was an animal of the same shape as the little green frogs he'd seen hopping around in the spring. Only this one was bigger and fatter, with warts. And it didn't hop, but just crouched slumpingly and fixed upon him its large cold, cold eyes. It was the same color as the dog.

On a low perch in the third cage was a rather large bird which Gummitch knew to be a parrot because the Mad Eunuch's owner kept a bright green one with a big yellow beak. But this one was mangy and ancient-looking and malevolent-eyed, while its wickedly curving beak pointed straight at him. Both its beak and its ragged feather coat were inky black.

The little dog coughed hackingly, and thunder crashed

outside as if the heavens were riven, while the great glare of lightning that simultaneously shone through the open doorway called Gummitch's attention to a fourth ebon beast just now hopped there and regarding him with an intelligence that seemed greater and more evil than that of the others.

It was an animal that Gummitch had never seen before, but thought because of its overlarge front top teeth must be related to squirrels, one of whom had terrified him in kittenhood when they'd first seen each other close from opposite sides of a window. And it had long, tall ears. Gummitch could only imagine it to be a deformed giant tailless squirrel, the product of mad science or vile sorcery.

Now it turned and, as lightning flared again and thunder crashed, hopped—to report, Gummitch was suddenly sure, to the cat doctor. The fearless cat-detective reached an instant decision and leaped down and raced after. The monstrous beast crossed the living room in four long hops, but Gummitch could readily match that speed, he found. In the front hall at the foot of the stairs, the beast turned at bay, making mewling sounds. Gummitch advanced on it stiff-legged and back arched, involuntarily letting out a loud and most undetectivelike caterwaul.

Then he saw beyond it the cat doctor coming down the stairs. She was stark naked, bore in her hand a long yellowish knife with a red hilt, and glared at him, the lips of her small mouth parted in a snarl that revealed her large front teeth.

He retreated to the living room. She came after, the knife advancing before her, followed by the black hopping giant squirrel-monster. Gummitch cast one longing look at the open window, but then remembered his responsibilities. To the accompaniment of the storm's hammer blows and flashes, he raced twice around the room to baffle them, then darted through the examination room back into the isolation ward.

93

They came after him relentlessly. From atop Psycho's cubicle he caterwauled defiance. They came up to it.

But then the storm's final and climatic thunder-crash and dazzling lightning-flare revealed to all three of them a new figure framed in the doorway, a rather small person wearing a dripping yellow oilskin and a deep-brimmed sou'wester.

It was Kitty-Come-Here, and she cried out, "Gummitch! I knew I'd find you here!"

Gummitch's fur relaxed a little. Wendy shoved the knife under some papers on the table beside her. The black squirrel-monster mewled innocently.

Kitty-Come-Here eyed the three of them in turn, taking her time about it, and then her gaze went on to the three occupants of the wire cages. At last she cried out comprehendingly, "Wendy, you are a *witch*. And that black rabbit there is your familiar. And although you claim this is a hospital for cats only, you've been treating or boarding the *familiars* of those three dreadful old women (all witches, of course; you probably have a whole coven!) in the Concordia in the room opposite my mother-in-law's. The resemblances are all unmistakable and prove my case. And when there's no outsider to see, you go around naked—"sky-clad" is your witch expression for that, isn't it? And you were chasing Gummitch and trying to do something to him, weren't you?"

Wendy reached a lab smock from a hook on the wall and shouldered into it leisurely. "Why, I never heard a more ridiculous set of ideas in my whole life," she said guilelessly. "It's true I sometimes bend the hospital's only-one-species rule a little, and it wouldn't do to advertise that to the mistresses of our guests. And I have a pet here, drop a curtsy, dear Bunnykins! Cats are wonderful, but one needs a break from them when one sees them all the time. And I do occasionally doctor or board pets of patients in the Concordia, both apt to be elderly for obvious reasons. Any psychologist will tell you, dear Helen, that people, especially elderly ones, grow to resemble their pets, or else select them with that point unconsciously in mind. I habitually sleep raw, and tonight when Bunnykins and I discovered loose in the hospital what we took to be a stray tom bent on raping (how could I know he was your Gummitch, dear?), we were seeking to eject him, that is all. There, does that answer your questions?"

"I don't think so," Helen said stoutly. "Why are all these animals *black,* I want to know? And what were you hiding when I came in?"

"I have a deep professional interest in melanism," Wendy told her. "And by the by, how *did* you get in?"

"When no one answered the door, I climbed through the open window, and now I'm glad I did! You still haven't told me—"

A joyous meow! from Gummitch interrupted this interchange. He was looking in Psycho's window. The young grey cat lifted her head a little and opened her eyes, which were no longer filmed with sickness, but bright with cat intelligence. She was smiling at Gummitch and them all. Though obviously still very weak and quite haggard-looking, she was clearly on the road to recovery.

This most happy occurrence rather put an end to serious accusations of witchcraft and other ill-feeling, and when Wendy insisted on serving them tea in a pot with an English Union Jack on it, with milk to go with it and seedcake, and with a saucer of milk for Gummitch, peace was fully sealed. Gummitch drank a third of his milk to please Kitty-Come-Here, though keeping a most wary eye on the cat doctor and Bunnykins, who appeared to resent that name, the cat judged, though continuing to act the innocent fool.

Afterward, going home by taxi, Helen told Gummitch,

"I still think she may be a witch, you know, but a rather nice one, just being kind to some dirty old sister witches—ugh, old as *Macbeth!* —and their sick animals. And she did have to admit you were most well-behaved, Gummitch, for a tom. I think that's a lot, coming from her. And you *did* uncover the whole thing, whatever it was, you know, you clever, sneaky cat. You broke through her British reticence, all right. She'd have played snob-doctor all night, otherwise. And did you notice, Gummitch, she had the slimmest and most stalwart body and the darlingest little breasts, almost as small as mine. I'm sure we're leaving Psycho in very good hands. But how should we tell Old Horsemeat about all this, Gummitch, when he comes back from his business-revels? Not everything, I think, though of course he'd love it all for one of his stories."

Gummitch decided she was still pretty featherbrained.

THRICE

THE

BRINDED

CAT

THRICE THE BRINDED CAT

Petite Helen Hunter and the tiger-striped family tom-cat, Gummitch, looked at each other solemnly from where they reposed at head and foot of the master bed, seeing witches. Those of Gummitch were dim, fire-lit prancing figures from the cat collective unconscious, which was like a prehistoric cave in his cat mind. His orangey short fur was of the pattern Shakespeare called brinded. He mewed once studiously.

The small, wise male cat was of two minds about the cat doctor and witch coven leader, Wendy Wicks. On the one hand, she threatened him with death, there was no denying. On the other, she had saved Psycho from the dreadful illness. Witches were the traditional friend of cats, his subconscious told him, so he was inclined to give her the benefit of the doubt, despite her monstrous familiar, Bunnykins.

Helen's witches made up a recognizable individualized coven of shapes, capering inside the white Victorian mansion that held the cat hospital. Leading them was Wendy Wicks, sometimes in robes, sometimes slenderly naked. Chief among her followers were three flitting elderly shapes, dimly accompanied by a fluttering parrot, a hopping toad, and a small hamster, all black. Observing them from a dimmer distance in Helen's subconscious was a family group, consisting of Helen's husband, Harry Hunter, his mother, Mrs. Hobart Hunter, bearing a crutch, and the Shakespearian actor, Hobart Hunter. The last of these had the staring yet unseeing eyes of death. The first figure, known to Gummitch as Old Horsemeat, let his gaze wander guiltily between his mother and his expired father. Harry's left hand, Helen saw now, held a half-drunk highball, which he sipped at constantly.

The real cat doctor, Wendy Wicks, joined Helen and Gummitch in the bedroom of their home.

"So it's the rapidity with which he reaches climax that makes the sexual behavior of your husband unsatisfactory?" the cat doctor and clinical psychologist asked.

"Oh, yes," Helen answered. "He's in and out like a flash. I can't believe he enjoys it. I certainly don't."

"It's the result, of course, of his alchoholism," the other responded.

"Only too true, I guess," Helen responded. He doesn't give me time to work up my feelings in response to his, before he's off again. He doesn't give me time to work up rhythmically."

The entire scene changed to the interior of the cat hospital. Mrs. Hobart Hunter entered, walking gingerly because of her recently healed hip. She was followed by a skinny, bent, elderly woman, bearing in her boney arms a bird cage wherein perched a black parrot. This one squawked a couple of raspy words, which seemed to be " 'Tis time, 'tis time."

Mrs. Hobart Hunter asked, "Was it three years back that we last played *Macbeth* in London City?"

The first witch answered, "No, it was only two years agone, for that was 1951, the year Parliament proclaimed witchcraft no longer a capital crime punishable by death."

The other responded eagerly, "Yes, yes, of course! For that decree was what enables us to suggest in our publicity that for the first time the witches in *Macbeth* would be portrayed by real witches appearing on the legitimate stage. If we had been a British company, we would have got more attention. Still, all considered, it worked out very well."

The second witch, a fat one, entered the scene, bear-

100

ing a frog, who croaked, "Anon, anon."

Harry Hunter, Old Horsemeat, entered the living room of the cat hospital, by way of the front door. He said gravely, "In 1949 my sainted father died. I was in Chicago at the time, and raced to the Coast by the fastest train. When I stood in the same room as his corpse I felt nothing but a strange fierce pride.

"I kept on with my drinking. My compulsion remained uncured."

He still bore in his hand the highball glass, from which he now drank measuredly.

He was followed, deviously, by the cat, Gummitch, who regarded the scene with Holmesian logic. He mewed again, somewhat didactically.

Downstairs came the third witch, a gliding mate to the other two, bearing in her skinny arms what first appeared to be a small dog, but was then seen to be a hamster of a blackish hue. While at the back of the room came Kitty-Come-Here and Wendy Wicks, both sky-clad, the latter followed by the black rabbit, Bunnykins. Wendy strode forward, Bunnykins beside her.

"Here beginneth," she entoned gravely, "the seventeenth session of the Four Square Coven, wherein Helen Hunter will be initiated to full fellowship."

As she continued her circling movement, Harry Hunter cut in ahead of her, saying, "I have been Helen's husband for all of seven years, and since she and you, high priestess, are both sky-clad (he indicated their nakedness with a gesture), I am emboldened to add that I have always loved her little breasts and was moved to honor them with my seed. But at the same time I must confess that I was equally enraptured by any pretty tits I have ever encountered. I venture to make these remarks because they seem to me to be very much to the point. I always thought wide sexual experience was expected of me, and I thought it a crying shame that I hadn't had it. I always worshipped breasts to a ridiculous degree. They seemed a sacrament to me, the outward sign of the inward glory of love. They were all-important. I didn't expect to say all this, but now it's said, I reaffirm it. Your breasts, for instance, o high priestess, are most engaging. If I have said too much, high priestess, I am sorry, but it's true."

Helen Hunter glared at him.

"It seems to me," she said, "that you have said a mouthful."

He replied, "A most delicious mouthful that would be."

Wendy Wick's high musical voice rang out.

"You had best shut up."

"It seemed to me a necessary declaration," Harry Hunter put in.

"Well, I never . . ." was the opinion of Mrs. Hobart Hunter, spoken with some horror. "It all seems to me most improper."

"The ceremony will continue," announced Wendy Wicks, "whatever to the contrary."

"Only after I have added this declaration," Harry Hunter persisted. "When Helen and I got married, her breasts were flat and pendulous, from tying them down to achieve a then-fashionable boyish figure. To tell you the truth, they quite horrified me. She had cosmetic surgery to repair them. This operation, somewhat dangerous, was entirely successful, as you can plainly see. I have never thanked her for her consideration and bravery, but I now do so. There! I've said all I was going to."

"It had better be," Helen put in.

"I shall now continue the ceremony," Wendy Wicks went on, "Making question of this voyager through space and time."

She faced Helen.

"Where howl winds fiercely?"

"Over Dunkery Beacon," Helen responded.

"Where break the waves wildly?" continued the first speaker.

"Upon Lulnorth Cove," the second responded.

"Where bites the bitter frost?"

"Upon White Nose Head."

"Where lingers the long night?"

"On Salisbury Plain."

"Where gathers the wet dawn?"

"On Winal Hill."

"Where shine the cold stars?"

"On Mendip Snows."

Standing there most erect, Wendy embraced Helen; their bodies joined length to length beautifully. They kissed each other.

Mrs. Hobart Hunter looked on in horror.

"Lesbianism!" she accused. "Harry! Harry! Your wife is being corrupted."

"Cool down, mother dear!" Harry interposed."I must applaud their good taste, since it is so exactly my own."

Wendy threw a challenging look at Mrs. Hunter, and kissed Helen again. They granted Harry Hunter a mixed glance, which was both defiant and mischievous.

"And may all your enemies be damned, my dearest," Wendy breathed.

Helen (somewhat flustered), "I'm overwhelmed by your attentions, dear high priestess, though Harry is still my husband, if he wants me."

"I'll say amen to all of that," said Harry Hunter. "My drinking has been hardest of all on you, my dear wife."

He inverted his glass so that the contents of the highball

splashed on the ground. He dropped the glass and set his foot on it. It broke with a resounding clash. From the depths the face of Hobart Hunter floated up, looking somewhat like William Shakespeare. In ghostly syllables he entoned:

> What a piece of work is man! How noble is reason!
> How infinite in faculties! In form and moving, how
> express and admirable! In action, how like an angel!
> In apprehension, how like a god! The beauty of the
> world! The paragon of animals!

"Was that last remark made in reference to me?" asked Gummitch. He mewed for the third time, with finality.

The kitten, Psycho, appeared suddenly, seemed to materialize beside the other cat. Gradually, the scene faded out.

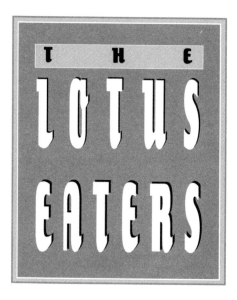

The Lotus Eaters

I always strongly disapproved of castrating male cats or spaying female ones—I believed that such operations diminished strength, invaded individuality, and were an insult to any being's right to procreate—until I started to take care of a house and three neutered cats in Summerland in Southern California. It was a lovely house on the dry, steep hillside.

Soon I began to have an understanding of my three eunuchs.

My wife spent most of her time in bed. She was ill and had an addiction for alcohol and books and soft fireside lights.

I fed the three cats: Braggi, a big, soft, sloppy male, red of hair and eye; Fanusi, a small beige female with the habits of a flapper; and the Grand Duchess, white with black spots, snakey and strong, who looked like some creature who should be riding point (though on what steed I don't know) before a troop of western cavalry.

Braggi was a lover. He would come over and just suddenly flop on my shoes—a great big gesture of affection.

Fanusi was a neurotic, despite her basic flapper behavior. Even while wooing you, she was nervous and apt to run off.

The Grand Duchess never lost her cool, though she was the smallest—yet hardiest—of the three.

The thing that most startled me about them, after about a week, was they they were all killers. They would bring in dead mice, rats even, birds and gophers, not eating them, but tossing them at my feet. I expected they were devoted exponents of blood sports. In fact, I noticed that the Grand Duchess had a regular hunting trail she took each day, waiting for a few minutes at each kill spot.

I wondered how they got enough to eat, since they apparently didn't eat their kills—merely displayed them to me, while their mistress, who owned the house, when strictly giving them into my trust, assured me that they each took only two teaspoons of canned cat food a day. A statement I immediately wondered about.

Soon I found the solution, through my wife, who understands people better than I do. Each of the three had a regular route to four sympathetic houses in the near neighborhood, where they got good victuals off the human tables.

Then I bacame more aware of the quite large garden on the downhill side of the house my wife and I were taking care of—along with the three desexed hunting cats. (Heck—desexed!) They even indulged often in sex play with each other—neutering isn't nearly such a disaster to sexual activity as many people think. Those three felines enjoyed each other.

I got still more interested in the garden downside of the house, from which the cries of the cats would sometimes come in the evenings like the soft coughs of lions.

The garden was a jungle. No, worse than a jungle. More like chaos.

So I started in on the worst stuff first. This happened to be a weed that had black spikes looking like early bamboo phonograph needles, but with tiny black burrs on the ends of them. They stuck on my socks and trousers very determinedly. But I kept getting rid of them, through the help of my wife.

Then I tackled a weed with small, brown, circular burrs. They weren't so troublesome to deal with. The back garden began to look like something I could conquer.

I started to cut out all sorts of dead wood. There were bushes that bore red berries in the center of the garden.

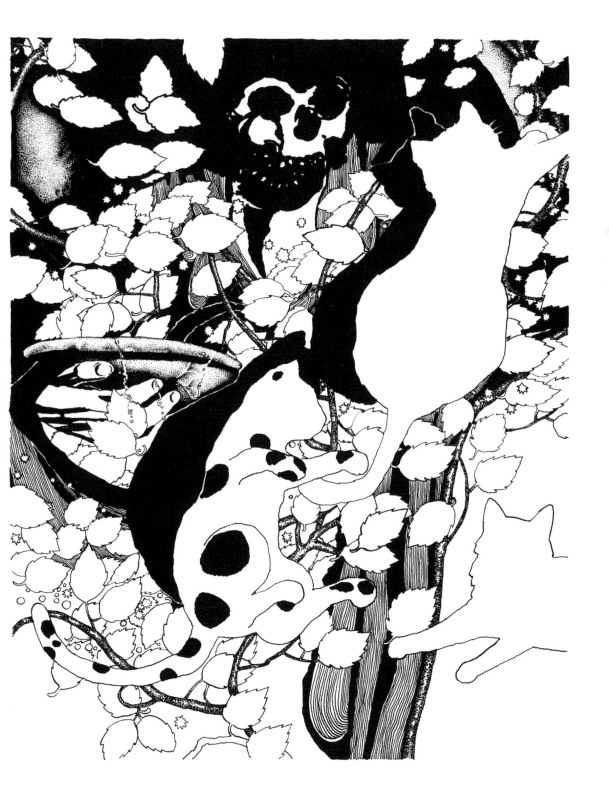

When I'd sawed all of their gray, dry, dead underwood away, I discovered a simple cement fountain underneath. I imagine the mistress and master of the house we were tending—along with their three cats—could hardly have known about the fountain, since for five years they had merely ground-hosed the garden from above a half hour every afternoon, their only attention to that area. I never did find out how that fountain worked.

My wife had a mild heart attack about that time, but we found her a doctor who did her good, and both she and I kept up our lonely ways of life, she in her bedroom, I at my typewriter in my study, and always for a strenuous, sweaty hour or three in the back garden.

I cleaned the lower surface out—now that the nastiest weeds were taken care of—first with a machete, then with a hand mower.

Then I began to get at the trees and the high border vegetation. This meant much more deadwood—too much for our garbage cans. I would load up my car with big corrugated cardboard boxes filled with my dead gray vegetable refuse and take it to the city dump, a huge dark valley behind the sea hills, but circled always with screaming sea birds. It gave me a strange feeling to do this, as if I were burying my wife—or one or all of the three cats she and I were tending.

At about this time Braggi started visiting me in the downhill garden while I worked. He would watch me closely, and when I sat down on the crude fountain edge to rest and wipe my face, he would topple against my ankles in affection. I would stroke him.

My wife read her books and drank her highballs in our bedroom. When she looked down at me from the wide window, it was companionably, affectionately, and concernedly. I would wave at her.

I was fascinated by the things my afternoon cuttings were uncovering. Working at the dead gray underbranches of two tall avocado trees, I discovered a complete hemispherical "pleasure dome," as in the poem by Coleridge, a dome walled overhead with huge green leaves and large green dropping fruit. My wife and I had a tremendous salad that night.

During later days, we gave away a number of these lovely, grainy-skinned fruits to briefly visiting friends.

At about this time the two "altered" female cats—the neurotic Fanusi and the stately Grand Duchess—began to look in on me and Braggi from a distance occasionally as I worked in the garden.

Then I attacked the fifteen-foot hedge of the whole garden—all green and vigorous with clumps of small yellow strange berries. I was amazed at my discoveries as I cut down this fierce stuff—three small evergreens growing sidewise in their attempt to get out of their huge green prison and reach the sun; two lovely branches of enormous, softly yellow roses just in bloom; and a small orange tree with tiny fruit.

That night my wife and I had a beautiful centerpiece at our dining table and lovely screwdrivers. I had a great feeling of triumph at having conquered the garden.

But later that night it was horrible. I awakened from a light sleep, and slipping out of the king-size bed very quietly, so as not to awaken my wife, I put on a dressing gown and stole down to the back garden.

Everything I had cut down was growing at a supernatural velocity, though I don't know what god or goddess had the power at that point.

For a moment I stood astounded—long enough to note Braggi, Fanusi, and the Grand Duchess watching me from the hillside, silhouetted by the moonlight.

It seemed clear that all the vegetation—grasses, weeds,

shrubs, vines, and trees—was determined to encircle and strangle to death me and my wife and the house.

I realized I had not a green thumb, to give life, but a gray thumb, to give death, though this left me with the paradox that in trying to bring the garden to life—to free it—I had infuriated it against me.

I rushed uphill and upstairs. My wife roused instantly. I grabbed a bottle for her. Without packing, we raced out to our car past threatening growing hedges and weeds which stung our legs. We jumped into the auto and started it, opening the back door and yelling, "Fanusi! Grand Duchess! Braggi! Pile in!"

To my relief and utter amazement they did—Fanusi almost in fits, Braggi loving as usual (in fact, snuggling up to my wife), the Duchess staring back over her white black-spotted shoulder in a proud way at the vegetation which appeared to be pursuing us.

Days later I sent some letters.

Three months afterward I heard from the couple who owned the house.

The chief points were that they were grateful to us for taking on their three cats—which had been a bother to them for a long time—but no offer to redeem their pets. And why had I left the back garden in such a rank state after promising to clear it? And yet taken away all the ripe avocados?

In view of which my plea for a little extra care-taking fee was ridiculous.

My wife and I looked at each other, while Braggi, Fanusi, and the Grand Duchess looked up at us from their appointed places before the flickering, red, streaming, mysterious fireplace, and smiled their Cheshire smiles.

CAT THREE

Skinny old Miss Skipsy kept and cherished three cats in her sixth-floor apartment, and their names were Cleopatra, Caesar and Mark Antony. She had heard of those plays written by Elizabeth Taylor and Claude Rains and Richard Burton. Or maybe those were the actors. She wasn't sure. Miss Skipsy wasn't sure about a lot of things, but about others she was devilishly certain—and frequently accurate.

Cleopatra and Caesar were seal point Siamese of the highest breed. They auraed the royal presence. They could readily have been exhibited at cat shows, but Miss Skipsy, who was basically an aristocrat and took for granted all cats were the same, never chose to do so.

Mark Antony was an alley cat of very dubious extraction. He looked most like a blue-cream American shorthair but was obviously impossibly mongrel by at least eighty points. He was *very* short-haired—"You went and got a crew cut again, Tony," Miss Skipsy used to reproach him lazily as she stroked his head—and he was one of the very few of the many cats whom Miss Skipsy had rescued from the foul streets and then taken to her skinny—truly, nonexistent—bosom. When a lady gets to her age, her womb and bosom both disappear, unless she be an inveterate hormones and silicone enthusiast.

Miss Skipsy was 78 and still a speed typist—137 words a minute for court stenographers who welcomed her deadly ability—and also able to make friends with all sorts of new people she met and be a Little Mother of All the World. She rescued loose or runaway dogs, horses, pigeons, and sea gulls (from whom she most carefully and with a great deal of medi-

117

cal know-how washed off the leaked crude oil that had driven them ashore), and of course she also rescued very many cats, and also men and women and marmosets, and other breeds of being. She would happily have rescued lions and tigers if given opportunity. Once she almost rescued a very neurotic black panther, used in the rites of some fearfully careless devil worshipers, but the police and their dreadful guns beat her by half a block.

She found homes for her foundlings amongst her friends, new acquaintances, and any decent-seeming persons she could browbeat into taking on an animal. Naturally she would never call the pound or the SPCA or any organization which would just kill them off after a brief period of offering them to some unknown person who wanted an unknown pet animal. She would rather have abandoned them in the big park by the seaside. But she always found homes for "her people," one way or another. (That was why she had to be a very speedy speed typist indeed, to finance her animal savings.)

She may even have rescued lost space folk for all we know from her brief memoirs and the obscure biogs of others—space people whose crafts had crashed and the like, the "Little Green Men" and all the others, including the ones that look and make sounds like Terran people and animals. She would have nursed them and when they got well released them in their own custody or shunted them off to her animal-loving friends or perhaps even tried to help them finance the repair or rebuilding of their spaceship, according to what they wanted and she thought best. It is a matter for deep speculation.

As we can certainly gather from the foregoing, Miss Skipsy was a bit of an authoritarian, but a loving and well-meaning one. She would mildly bawl out Caesar for biting by the slack of the neck and trying to rape his mother

Cleopatra—he really should have been called Caesarean—
with Mark Antony interestedly looking on. Nothing would
ever have "happened" in the sense of impregnation or even
intercourse, because Cleo and Caesar had long since been
neutered, an act for which Miss Skipsy alternately castigated
and praised herself.

At least it was a step against a cat population explosion,
and we do have about 22 million domestic cats in the USA.
And for that matter many humans are allowing and even
encouraging the explosion of many populations, including
their own. But here I get too close to the language of Miss
Skipsy, who strictly believed in neutering male and female
cats—and humans too, after the woman had borne two children, or else the male had been cited even once in a pater-
nity suit.

Not a bad idea—Malthus and Heinlein can't *always* be
right.

So we have the three cats who live in their one-room-
plus-bath apartment. Cleopatra, who was 16 years old, older
than Miss Skipsy, comparatively, rheumy-eyed and shedding
seal point hairs like mad. Mark Antony took to grooming her
regularly, which Miss Skipsy was too busy, and Caesar too crazy
to do except upon occasion, and it kept down Cleo's hairballs
and asthmatic coughing.

Caesar, cross-eyed, mad-masked, and wild. Cleo the
crone. And Mark Antony, watching them both and making
up to Miss Skipsy. He was the most empathetic of the cats, with
the greatest insight into their, and even his own, behavior. He
also had a diet problem. He refused the chopped kidney and
dry food Miss Skipsy gave Cleo and Caesar and took only liquid food from Miss Skipsy. Breast milk—no, of course, but
Miss Skipsy secretly mixed vitamins, liver extracts, and pro-
tein powders into the liquid foods he favored. Sometimes he

tasted them and gave her a reproachful glance, yet kept on lapping.

Antony had a constant eye on Caesar, but who could tell what that meant?

Caesar had never been out of the room in which he had been born except for brief scampers down the corridor toward the elevator. He believed that the room was the Cosmos—with a tiny and mysterious connection to infinity, the Corridor. He also frequently looked out the big window, which was French type and swung. Miss Skipsy kept it tied about three inches open with an old bandeau which she had worn when she was a champion tennis player. Caesar thought all outside there was a weird part of his brain. But where did those birds come from? Frightening, even to a cat, to have birds in one's belfry.

Cleo knew it wasn't imaginary because she had her childhood memories of life in gardens. While Antony knew it very well because of his alley cat life. But Caesar really believed it—that eternity and immortality (and flight!—and all the other imagining of his crook-eyed brain) were just outside the window, sixth floor.

Miss Skipsy loved them all. She talked to all three of them—wild insights with Caesar, mild Hindi conclusions with Cleo, and rather drier ideas with Antony, who was an extremely logical cat, providing logic agreed with what he wanted. She loved all of them—they were her family, as opposed to the people she merely loved and helped.

She was a great gal. She devoted five days a week to loving two- and four-legged people with almost telepathic empathy and one secret hour to hating them, and 47 hours to feeling guilty.

But by a shade Antony had the better telepathy. He knew Caesar was fringe-psychotic and was very much inter-

MISS SKIPSY...

ested in him for that reason. He knew Cleo was fringe-senile—and treasured her for that reason. He knew Miss Skipsy had the cat equivalent of a very high IQ, and he was very pleased with her for that reason.

Empathy in cats—particularly the intense empathy that goes with ESP—is quite a problem. To start with, they don't even like each other so much. Oh, they are attracted to and make use of each other, and they admire each other endlessly, as they do all beauty. But empathy deep and true between them? Rare.

So, naturally, empathy between a cat and a human, a horse, a dog, a soft-spoken extraterrestrial, or any other creature is rarer still, taking at least as much patience and skill as manning a falcon. Naturally, most sane cats will give polite thanks when a food offering is made. They prefer the finest peoplefood; next, the best catfood; but they will eat stinking fish if absolutely necessary—though a few pampered and irrealistic blue bloods dragged down to such a situation would rather starve.

As for inanimate objects, absolutely no empathy whatsoever! Though especially if it be of an interestingly pleasant texture, they will *admire* such an object as much as they admire any beautiful being, or—almost—a goddess. But if it doesn't strike their sense of beauty, they will take even less notice of it than a king does of a beggar.

This is one of the reasons cats expect cars to get out of their way when they stride across the street, which quite a few cars don't. The soul of a car is tiny and hidden in a deep, dark and malodorous place.

In this, cats are like their chief goddess, Bast, although neither the cat nor the goddess knows this, at least at gut level. Crossing a modern boulevard, Bast would have her corporeal form destroyed not seven but a thousand times.

No, cats expect all cars, from Rolls-Royces to Fords to trucks, to get out of their way—they never even attack cars like dogs, cars being beneath contempt—and if they don't step fast, they generally get it, except if they encounter a cat-fond motorist, who will risk a dangerous accident rather than killing one of the divine dears.

Cats have a collective subconscious, as posited by Carl Jung for man, going back to the saber-toothed tiger at least, and culminating in the glorious day when a short-haired, yellow-and-brown-striped Kaffir cat first strode into a neat primitive Egyptian village and said, in effect, "Here I am. I catch rats and mice. I'm friendly if treated with courtesy. Gimme some meat or milk."

Oh yes, cats remember all that, as you can see from their slitted, ever-watchful eyes. Way back to Egypt and well beyond—to the day when felines decided, partly because of their short intestines, almost incapable of assimilating a vegetarian diet, to eat the blood and flesh of their own mammalian criminals forever and ever, though of course they were just getting into the cat race, usually named after a more malodorous mammal.

Cats mostly just pretend to love humans, but if there's one thing they really love, it's gardens. They like to brush against flowers rather than weeds. They have fine taste.

But most cats also have claustrophilia. They will stay in one room endlessly—as Caesar, not even demanding a private garden. Or if shut in a dressing drawer, especially one with nice clean sweet linen or silk to lie on, they will recline there for hours and hours without a cry. Maybe they are the first people of the Black or Dark World, loving it all the time. But perhaps fresh linen is what cats love most. I have seen two enemy cats lie closely side by side on a freshly washed, nubbly bedspread.

So for them durance vile is not so vile, provided it is velvet-lined.

Antony, because of his alley cat peculiarities, got his liquid food anywhere in the house he wanted it, which was a nice attention from Miss Skipsy. She was a good and convivial girl.

Antony got to watching Caesar more and more. He had a cat-scientific curiousity. And Caesar, being a crazy character, was basically interesting. So Antony watched. Actually the Siamese Caesar spooked him and made his collective subconscious go back to the late Middle Ages when they were apt to kill any cat as a witch's familiar. Brr!

Caesar was really a crazy cat. For instance, he ignored his bowl of dry cat food and did great thieving operations to get and open the box of this same dry cat food three shelves up in the kitchen cupboard. Truly a cat burglar. Antony would willingly have joined him in his nefarious activities, but there was no profit to him in them, and Caesar would have resented it deeply and perhaps dangerously.

Caesar used to watch from the window at the world he believed to be part of his own brain. But only by day.

Miss Skipsy had very dark drapes and kept them closely drawn all through the night. The three cats enjoyed that too— Caesar because then he could stop watching his own mind outside the window and go to sleep.

Antony, the short-haired mongrel, kept smelling Caesar by night and watching him by day.

Antony had rather human habits, which somewhat pleased Miss Skipsy, such as avoiding the sandbox and sitting carefully on the edge of the toilet "to do his business." Perhaps an earlier owner had trained him in this action before his alley-catting days.

The reason Miss Skipsy served Antony anywhere in the apartment was because he was so meticulous in lapping up his liquid foods, without spilling a drop, while Caesar and Cleo ate in the bathroom.

Despite Caesar's skill in getting at filched dry cat food (he chewed off the corners of the cardboard boxes), he couldn't for all his genius, open tin cans. Impossible unless someone opens a cat factory where steel mittens are made to fit claws and paws.

Antony kept on watching Caesar as Caesar kept watch on the hallucinatory but dreadfully real and tempting birds, birds that seemed (in his brain- or apartment-Cosmos) to be flying nearer and nearer to Miss Skipsy's window, sometimes so close he couldn't resist mewing invitingly, or starting backwards with a snarl, or even leaping suddenly at the glass— which repulsed him. Antony saw in all this behavior evidence of ambivalence and a growing psychosis, though he lacked sufficient insight to realize that, to Caesar, everything outside the window was happening in Caesar's mind. Antony became madly curious as to how it would all end, and now *his* bad side came out.

One afternoon when Miss Skipsy was out and the birds were wheeling noisily close in the hot sunlight, Antony with heartless alley cat impulse and cunning clipped through the bandeau which kept the window open its cat-proof three inches. The window swung wide.

Caesar leaped for a passing bird—and violently out into the yawning space. He missed the bird, but cat reflexes taking over instantly, he landed lightly on the sanded tar of the opposite roof seven feet beyond the window sill. Two hours later Miss Skipsy came, saw, and rescued him, then attended to a darker and bloodier matter, involving an unpleasant session with the police, from which she emerged victorious.

It was really too bad about Antony. In leaping to rescue Caesar, or perhaps merely *imitate* Caesar's escape, he fell short

125

and was smashed on the cement six floors below.

Poor Antony! He had tripped on the old hairbrush with which he groomed Cleo and also on the screwdriver, half vodka and half orange juice, he had been drinking. Also, his mass was about that of a jaguar rather than a house cat, and so instead of walking away like an ant from his fall, or limping away like a mouse, or conceivably recovering like a house cat, he was smashed—fortunately skull-first, so that he died almost instantly.

While falling, he had time to scream unheard: "Idiot! Drunken sponger!"

The Bump

*Owned by a pair of Siamese, I find it easy to empathize with
those who think the planet is going to the dogs . . .*

Pursuing came that dreadful, horrendous, moron
BOW-WOW. Why should the apartment next door have such a
maniac? A poodle, a fox terrier, a Saint Bernard, even a blood-
hound or German Shepherd would have been preferable. I
controlled my prejudices, which are pretty strong, and looked
around. A Doberman Pinscher, next door it had to be,
emblem of fascism.

All my underclothes were on the floor except for those
which, perchance, I was wearing. Kim, the darling, had been
busy. He had cleaned out the two top drawers in the dresser
of my one-room apartment. He loves me, no question, and
also is something of a fetishist. Though that's odd, since his
species doesn't wear clothes. Oh well, maybe he's a sweat
fetishist.

Clawing with his claws, he'd opened those two top drawers. And then dragging with his paws—he is never a cat to
damage things, except occasionally me out of pure if savage
affection—he had drawn out all the lingerie. Queer karma for
a cat—probably he's the reincarnation of a dirty old man. Or
a dirty young one. Born under the sign of Leo, anyhow, as I've
calculated. Cats such as Kim have a nicety about such matters
as their birthday.

But no real strategy or tactics, at least toward the one
they love. Just as now, guiltily but most conspicuously, Kim
had hidden, snaking shrewdly, under the blanket of my bed.
Because of which behavior he has a second name: The Bump.

He really looks quite comic, innocently bulging under the blanket like six or so bananas. But I'd never tell him that. Until they are completely empathized and instructed—something impossible until they are older than Kim—cats are extremely sensitive, outrageously touchy. Much more so than dogs, who take out their sensitivity by fawning, slavish, "Please beat me" behavior—the master masochists of the universe. But never cats, who were very aristocratic Gods in their day—Egyptian Bast, etc. And they somehow keep living up to it, even now when the uninstructed ones are speechless. A long-enduring breed with a high resistance to mutation.

Such were my thoughts as I took off my coat, dress, shoes, silk tights, and underclothes, tossing the last in the pile Kim the Bump had made. Stripping down to my own short, scanty, red-gold hair. I really am a sentimentalist and after all Kim and I are, from quite away back, comrades, buddies, chums. He even goes to the movies with me, quiet as a mouse inside my coat—though God knows what he sees in them— they're just one (and about the dullest) of my anthropological assignments.

About that time, Fatimah waddled out of the bathroom. She—Kim's mother—can do a four-foot vertical jump, but being fifteen years old and rather overweight, she never demonstrates this amazing ability to spectators, except in cases of utter emergency. Or when, rarely, her mind wanders. Then she jumps five feet. She is completely empathized and instructed. She is, poor dear, somewhat senile, but being ladies we understand each other perfectly. After all, I empathized and instructed her. We are friends—and Kim too, except he's a beatnik, poor dog-type cat. Out of Siam. Whence strange things come, I gather.

Kim, the Bump, bit my ankle quite deeply—a sign that I was going to have to make a star decision quite soon.

Although unempathized and uninstructed, Kim the Bump is strong on instinct.

Fatimah glanced at Kim, but did not approach him. He has an Oedipus Complex (as they call it on this planet) to astound Oedipus (some fabulous ancient Greek) whom Sophocles—another ancient Greek—(damn the bunch of them!) wrote about interminably. Anyhow, Fatimah kept well away from Kim. Which habit may well have given her stability, her four-footedness on reality. Kim has never been out of this room all his life. Unlike Fatimah, who was out her first three years. I imagine Kim thinks of this room as the universe, with everything else—seen through the windows, spied through the door—illusion. (Sometimes he does run out of the door down the hall, but it is red-carpeted and he likely thinks of it as Hell. Window-Heaven with its swift, bird-painted illusions and Hall with its Human-haunted Hell.)

While I was wondering these things, I was looking at my naked, bony, six-foot body in the ceiling-to-floor, whore-house type mirror—the only extravagance I permit myself on this planet. I have a feeling for the economies of Galaxy Center, if no one else has. My sign, like Kim's, is Leo. I come from a near-by sun. My gaze centered on my firm, flat breasts, with nipples large as big, narrowing strawberries. I was not in the least put down by the absence there of bulging milk-sacks. On this planet I have learned that many men go for just such a figure as mine—*Playboy* and the comics (so rightly named!) and doctors indoctrinated with breast-feeding to the contrary. Perhaps the men viewing me (and girls perchance, who knows?) desire something excitingly neuter. Hermaphrodites, etc.

Still, despite these interesting thoughts, I was getting awfully sick of Terra, as those aforementioned ancient Greeks called it, who were about the best folk on the whole orb, past or present, I'd judge. Since then it's been a typical case (let me snooze my nose) of recession, degeneration, and plain "Let's go to Hell" business. Even the Greeks, in their own country, have become a bunch of incredible, torturing no-goods. More sadistic even than Kim, who just bit my ankle again. Ah, well, it's all okay. Fatimah is all set to send the sub-ether message to Galaxy Center from her sub-station. Under the incredibly floor-cluttered lowest table. Oh, what a mess! We cats are most neat about our excretia and bodies (just now I'm licking my somewhat scanty short red fur). But nothing else—confusion entire! Except perhaps our thoughts. Still, I'm not certain about those. They may be all mixed up.

The blue light sparked (I had drawn the curtains, shutting out hateful Sol) and I dictated to Fatimah while Kim crouched in a dark corner (I've taught Fatimah Galaxy Center Code and I'm a lazy one), "Scrub this planet, as far as feline migration is concerned. It's dog, dog, dog, dog, dog, dog, dog. No place—no hidey-holes even—for individuality. At the least, 43 per cent dog, or 1, 111, 110, or even 99 percent, as they call it on this slavish, flattering, ultimately always doggy, forever decimal planet. Unless you answer in two minutes (their time), I'll off to Mars (fourth planet, Sol, their war-god name), though I gather it's a washout too. *Men* have been there. And on their moon too.

"Incidentally," I said, "I'm taking Fatimah and Kim with me—their names, our people. Our kind, though partial-primitive. If there's anything a cat is, it's self-willed—and most whimsical."

Kim, the Bump, bit my ankle a third time.

THE

GREAT
SAN FRANCISCO
GLACIER

Twenty seconds before the Twenty Minute War struck, Seward Suess, the world's wealthiest mystery man, took up a pair of shears of gold alloyed with molybdenum for hardness and smartly clipped the taut blue ribbon. Instantly there went into operation the deep-level solar-electric system that distributed electricity from sun-power generators spotted all over the Mojave Desert to various sections of Arizona, Nevada, Utah, and California.

The fifty genius-level scientists and engineers who had designed the system dutifully applauded. They had been lured by Suess to Las Vegas on the promise of infinite opportunity for investigating the statistics of games of chance, dancing girls, and large fortunes.

As the blue ribbon-ends popped apart and subsided toward the seamless red carpet covering the vast patio, Seward Suess had one of those instantaneous intuitions which had previously saved him from earthquakes, hurricanes, and hit men hired by his wealthy mystery enemies on the rare occasions when he had ventured forth from one of his hiding holes into the hyper-dangerous outer world.

Without a word or a moment's hesitation he sprinted toward the gleaming door of the elevator which would convey him down by swift stages into the impregnable subterranean retreat—twice as deep, he reminded himself complacently, as the bombproof which ensured the safety of the President of the United States. It would be empty now—he never allowed a soul to remain below when he ventured aloft—but empty or not, it would guard.

His fifty genius-level hirelings went on applauding, oblivious to the sudden departure of their employer, or else rating it as one more charming eccentricity.

His eight bodyguards did take note, but they were also taken for a moment by surprise. Belatedly they sprinted after their fleeting boss.

The genius-level hirelings increased their applause, as if the chase were some delightful impromptu vaudeville.

Seward Suess, maintaining his lead, neared the silvery door and the gold button beside it. One punch and the door would snap open, and he would be surging toward safety—and *without* his bodyguards, as he intended. Dilatory henchmen deserved their dooms.

Meanwhile, deep in the bunker—which was *not* altogether deserted—in fact, in its deepest room, Suess's study, there patiently waited Mr. Dark, his face pale and composed as marble. Mr. Dark had entered the bunker through its secret escape tunnel. He was the world's most mystery assassin and cunningest compulsive murderer, hired by Seward Suess's most mystery enemy. Yet Mr. Dark would never have accepted the assignment had it not appealed to him as a problem deserving the aesthetic solution which his unique professional skills could achieve. Mr. Dark was accompanied only by his faithful albino Doberman pinscher, High Noon, as composed as and even more pallid than himself.

Seward Suess, still holding a commanding lead over his henchmen, shot out his finger toward the golden target of the button which would hurry him down and away from an appointment in Samarra.

But sometimes even Death anticipates himself.

Three suns dawned simultaneously. They were brighter than tropical noontide, cubed, and evenly spaced around the horizon. With barely time to think that he was a fool to have dared Fate, again, and that—yes!—his intuitions were always right, Seward Suess became incandescent powder along with his eight bodyguards and fifty genius-level hirelings. Within seconds, practically all human beings and other animals, whether genius-level or inbecile, were destroyed from San Diego to West Berlin, victims of a brilliant first strike by Sino-Russian nuclear rockets. But hardly seconds later, in a massive retaliation by Americo-European intercontinental ballistic missiles, launched on first suspicion, there were wiped out most of the population and all the industrial potential of Asia and Russia.

The Suess bunker was shaken to its roots. Mr. Dark raised his eyebrows at the impertinence of this rude tossing, while High Noon silently snarled back his thin pink lips, though otherwise the genius-level hit dog remained as poker-faced as his master.

Everything in America was surface-destroyed (even parts of the Rocky Mountains) except the Mojave Desert, which didn't seem worth hydrogen bombs. So the deep-level solar-electric system kept operating after the obliteration of the rest of industrial America. However, the distribution system was fatally damaged, except for one deep underground electrical power conduit leading to San Francisco.

But San Francisco had been destroyed, leveled much more thoroughly than by the earthquake and fire of 1906, except for one six-story apartment building at Geary and Hyde streets, which stayed upright because it was at the point of intersection of two lines where northern and southern bomb blasts, and also eastern and western ones, canceled each other out. All the people in this apartment building died from radiation except for one very *zaftig* yet svelte young lady named Jane on the fifth floor, who was protected by her excessive baby fat from the radiation, along with her two Siamese cats, Fatima and Kim, who were crouched under her protecting body at doomsday time. Also, Jane firmly believed in astrol-

137

ogy, and all her planets were in their very best houses at the evil moment.

Hers was the only apartment building now able to use the electricity from the deep-level system which kept shooting out nearly infinite power from the Mojave. Several other apartments (those ahead on their rent) in the same building were still getting electricity from the deep-level system and so although their occupants were dead, their refrigerators were not.

After about three days Jane came out of her apartment to seek food for herself and her cats, who aristocratically stayed at home, expecting their mistress to solve all their difficulties.

She managed to find, amidst the rubble of nearby groceries and supermarkets, a number of edible canned human dinners and a lot of dry and canned catfood, more resistant to damage than human food.

Meanwhile Mr. Dark had emerged from the secret tunnel by which he had entered the Suess bunker, after High Noon had sniffed the outer air and signified by a curt nod to his master that it was fall-out free. The hit man gazed around at the utter devastation, nodded solemnly, and might have smiled except that a thought too deep for quick recognition began to trouble his upper mind.

High Noon also gazed around, but more like a questing radar. His muzzle, after a few experimental swings past and back, settled down pointing northwest. Still preoccupied with the elusive thought, Mr. Dark nodded somewhat absently, and together they began to trudge northwest across the ashen waste which was almost as colorless as they.

A week of travel carried them to the congenial purlieus of Death Valley. They might have starved except for a rush of white animals hurrying south in a sudden lemming-sprint toward destruction—arctic foxes, white wolves, ermine, at last polar bears—only a few at first, but slowly increasing in numbers. Mr. Dark regularly shot one of the towering bears down, and he and High Noon shared the raw livers between them, washing down the organ meat with blood.

"Eat the liver, High," Mr. Dark would say somberly. "It is the vital food—and, on occasion, the lights."

In Death Valley they might have lingered. Mr. Dark knelt down and threw his arm around his loyal dog. "It's our kind of place, High," he muttered with unusual loquacity and affection. "The perfect name." He seemed lost in a dream. High Noon shook off the arm, not unfriendly, and continued hit-doggedly on his way. Mr. Dark's pale-irised eyes glazed. His elusive thought had reached consciousness: No matter how charming in itself, worldwide death wasn't an adequate substitute for the joys of compulsive, unending murder. He must find human beings to kill, if humanly possible, or else go mad. He got to his feet and took up the northwestward trudge at High Noon's heels.

In San Francisco, Jane was having to forage further and further to support herself and her feline friends. From this exercise she grew slim as Marlene Dietrich and indeed began closely to resemble this film star—a tremendous sex-target if there had been any man left to see her. She became bony and super-elegant, and she sometimes picked up *Vogue*-style dresses from the remnants of ladies' clothing stores.

At about this time her refrigerator, operating on super-power from the Mojave, began to exert its full force. The accumulating ice burst open its door and pressed out in a solid glacial front studded with TV dinners, lettuce heads shrunken and turned brown, sausage ends, broken eggs, and tiny mysteries wrapped in tinfoil.

After a few efforts to quell the ice with hot water which

no longer ran hot, the *zaftig* and svelte Jane, now bony and beautiful, moved out into the corridor, and her frightened cats with her—it was the first time Kim and Fatima had ventured out of the apartment in all their lives.

Jane thought despairingly of the frozen beef stroganoff and chopped chicken livers and chicken chow mein she had been saving up, but they were embedded in the face of the ceiling-high glacier now coming from her refrigerator.

The ice had broken open, by sheer mass, the apartment door, pushed down the corridor, and begun to go down the stairway and the elevator shaft and the fire escape, remorselessly evicting the beautiful gaunt woman and her cats from their temporary camps. Then there came ominous thudding crashes as other apartment doors were burst open and added their ice to Jane's, her glacier having had the start of theirs because she never defrosted, while the others had automatic defrosters which functioned sporadically.

High Noon and Mr. Dark skirted the roots of Mount Whitney and continued their northwestward trudge between King's Canyon Park and Yosemite. They continued to live on the livers of fresh-killed white beasts, especially the large and invigorating livers of polar bears. But Mr. Dark's psychic hunger for human murderees continued to mount.

In San Francisco, Jane, Kim and Fatima fled desperately from their glacier-stuffed building.

The ice mounted up at the intersection of Geary and Hyde streets and began moving toward Market Street, Golden Gate Park, the Golden Gate Bridge, the Pacific Ocean, the Nimitz Freeway, Twin Peaks, Hunter's Point, and in other directions. Jane, Fatima, and Kim retreated reluctantly southward, living by preference on the ice rather than ahead of it. The two cats learned to forage for themselves; their fur lengthened; they grew rangey, bony, and iron-thewed as their mistress.

Then one frosty, sun-dazzled morning near San Jose they saw on the next ridge ahead of them two strange figures more chilling than the ice—a huge snow-white dog and, close beside, a tall, skeletally thin man clad in black, but with a visage pallid as the world around him. Yet both the man and dog weaved as they walked. The scene was eerie, closely resembling a solarized photograph.

The man pointed a black-tipped white hand toward them, and chips of ice flew up between Jane and Kim, where a missile had gouged it. The three comrades dropped prone and began fearlessly to squirm forward, stalking their suddenly-appeared foes.

Doubtless, despite their courage, they would have fallen to the gun of the man and the fangs of the dog. But when Jane reached the former and the two Siamese the latter, both Mr. Dark and High Noon were writhing in the agonies of death, poisoned at last by the excess of vitamin A in the polar bear livers that had been for weeks the staple of their diet. Mr. Dark's last thought was that, had his hand not been shaky from disease, he would never have missed this most murderworthy girl creeping toward him, wavy as the outlines of a dream.

Jane, Kim and Fatima got to their feet and paws and went on.

The Mojave power-sources kept working most efficiently. Gradually the San Francisco Glacier occupied the whole Bay and kept spreading. A copy of the *Bay Guardian* headlined "Defend Our Bay" traveled a long way with it. Oddly, the *Bay Guardian* had called public attention to all sorts of pollution, but never pollution by ice.

Thirty years later, the South Americans—Spaniards and Incas becoming independent of each other during the course of the Long Terror—began cautiously to move northward across the narrow and volcano-ridden ribbon of Panama and over the blasted remains of Central America and Mexico. They wrapped their ponchos more closely around them as they got their first breath of chill from the San Francisco Glacier. Shortly they encountered a population of fierce arcticized Siamese cats led by a beautiful bony white goddess, a goddess of fire and ice, of glaciers and volcanoes, a true Pali-Kali type. The cats had learned to talk, or at least to hiss most threateningly and variously with a strong suggestion of true speech.

The two forces made peace and set up boundaries. So did the similar forces on the opposite sides of the Atlantic and Pacific.

Gradually, the great Antarctic continental glacier melted, as did earth's northern ice cap, due to the competition of the Great San Francisco Glacier. Many cities were drowned, but not San Francisco, which effectively froze all the water, salt or sweet, that rose against it.

The earth, disturbed by the new distribution of mass, flipped over so that San Francisco was its new north pole, and a point in the Indian Ocean its south pole. This latter began to accumulate its ice.

The Mojave electricity source, now operating 500 miles from the north pole, continued to work quite efficiently despite the subarctic climate. Jane removed herself and her increasingly intelligent and more numerous Siamese cats there, and together they started a new culture.

It was (except for the Siamese cats and their white goddess and the equally resourceful Koreans and koala bears and Lilliputians and lemmings on the other two sides of the globe) . . .

THE END

SHIP OF SHADOWS

"Issiot! Fffool! Lushshsh!" hissed the cat and bit Spar somewhere.

The fourfold sting balanced the gut-wretchedness of his looming hangover, so that Spar's mind floated as free as his body in the blackness of Windrush, in which shone only a couple of running lights dim as churning dream-glow and infinitely distant as the Bridge or the Stern.

The vision came of a ship with all sails set creaming through blue, wind-ruffled sea against a blue sky. The last two nouns were not obscene now. He could hear the whistle of the salty wind through shrouds and stays, its drumming against the taut sails, and the creak of the three masts and all the rest of the ship's wood.

What was wood? From somewhere came the answer: plastic alive-o.

And what force flattened the water and kept it from breaking up into great globules and the ship from spinning away, keel over masts, in the wind?

Instead of being blurred and rounded like reality, the vision was sharp-edged and bright—the sort Spar never told, for fear of being accused of second sight and so of witchcraft.

Windrush was a ship too, was often called the Ship. But it was a strange sort of ship, in which the sailors lived forever in the shrouds inside cabins of all shapes made of translucent sails welded together.

The only other things the two ships shared were the wind and the unending creaking. As the vision faded, Spar began to hear the winds of Windrush softly moaning through the long passageways, while he felt the creaking in the vibrant shroud to which he was clipped wrist and ankle to keep him from floating around in the Bat Rack.

Sleepday's dreams had begun good, with Spar having Crown's three girls at once. But Sleepday night he had been half-waked by the distant grinding of Hold Three's big chewer. Then werewolves and vampires had attacked him, solid shadows diving in from all six corners, while witches and their familiars tittered in the black shadowy background. Somehow he had been protected by the cat, familiar of a slim witch whose bared teeth had been an ivory blur in the larger silver blur of her wild hair. Spar pressed his rubbery gums together. The cat had been the last vision of the ship.

His hangover hit him suddenly and mercilessly. Sweat shook off him until he must be surrounded by a cloud of it. Without warning his gut reversed. His free hand found a floating waste tube in time to press its small trumpet to his face. He could hear his acrid vomit gurgling away, urged by a light suction.

His gut reversed again, quick as the flap of a safety hatch when a gale blows up in the corridors. He thrust the waste tube inside the leg of his short, loose slopsuit and caught the dark stuff, almost as watery and quite as explosive as his vomit. Then he had the burning urge to make water.

Afterwards, feeling blessedly weak, Spar curled up in the equally blessed dark and prepared to snooze until Keeper woke him.

"Sssot!" hissed the cat. "Sssleep no more? Sssee? Sssee shshsharply!"

In his left shoulder, through the worn fabric of his slopsuit, Spar could feel four sets of prickles, like the touch of small thorn clusters in the Gardens of Apollo or Diana. He froze.

"Sspar," the cat hissed more softly, quitting to prickle. "I wishsh you all besst. Mosst ashshuredly."

Spar warily reached his right hand across his chest, touched short fur softer than Suzy's, and stroked gingerly.

The cat hissed very softly, almost purring. "Ssturdy Sspar! Ssee ffar! Ssee fforever! Fforessee! Afftssee!"

Spar felt a surge of irritation at this constant talk of see-ing—bad manners in the cat!—followed by an irrational surge of hope about his eyes. He decided that this was no witch cat left over from his dream, but a stray which had wormed its way through a wind tube into the Bat Rack, setting off his dream. There were quite a few animal strays in these days of the witch panic and the depopulation of the Ship, or at least of Hold Three.

Dawn struck the Bow then, for the violet forecorner of the Bat Rack began to flow. The running lights were drowned in a growing white blaze. Within twenty heartbeats Windrush was bright as it ever would be on Workday or any other morn-ing.

Out along Spar's arm moved the cat, a black blur to his squinting eyes. In teeth Spar could not see, it held a smaller grey blur. Spar touched the latter. It was even shorter furred, but cold.

As if irked, the cat took off from his bare forearm with a strong push of hind legs. It landed expertly on the next shroud, a wavery line of grey that vanished in either direction before reaching a wall.

Spar unclipped himself, curled his toes round his own pencil-thin shroud, and squinted at the cat.

The cat stared back with eyes that were green blurs which almost coalesced in the black blur of its outsize head.

Spar asked, "Your child? Dead?"

The cat loosed its grey burden which floated beside its

head.

"Chchchchild!" All the former scorn and more were back in the sibilant voice. "It izzzz a rat I sssslew her, isssssiot!"

Spar's lips puckered in a smile. "I like you, cat. I will call you Kim."

"Kim-shlim!" the cat spat. "I'll call you Lushshsh! Or Sssot!"

The creaking increased, as it always did after dayspring and noon. Shrouds twanged. Walls crackled.

Spar swiftly swivelled his head. Though reality was by its nature a blur, he could unerringly spot movement.

Keeper was slowly floating straight at him. On the round of his russet body was mounted the great, pale round of his face, its bright pink target-center drawing attention from the tiny, wide-set, brown blurs of his eyes. One of his fat arms ended in the bright gleam of pliofilm, the other in the dark gleam of steel. Far beyond him was the dark red aft corner of the Bat Rack, with the great gleaming torus, or doughnut, of the bar midway between.

"Lazy, pampered he-slut," Keeper greeted. "All Sleepday you snored while I stood guard, and now I bring your morning pouch of moonmist to your sleeping shroud.

"A bad night, Spar," he went on, his voice growing sententious. "Werewolves, vampires, and witches loose in the corridors. But I stood them off, not to mention rats and mice. I heard through the tubes that the vamps got Girlie and Sweetheart, the silly sluts! Vigilance, Spar! Now suck your moonmist and start sweeping. The place stinks."

He stretched out the pliofilm-gleaming hand.

His mind hissing with Kim's contemptuous words, Spar said, "I don't think I'll drink this morning, Keeper. Corn gruel and moonbrew only. No, water."

"What, Spar?" Keeper demanded. "I don't believe I can

allow that. We don't want you having convulsions in front of the customers. Earth strangle me!—what's that?"

Spar instantly launched himself at Keeper's steel-gleaming hand. Behind him his shroud twanged. With one hand he twisted a cold, thick barrel. With the other he pried a plump finger from a trigger.

"He's not a witch cat, only a stray," he said as they tumbled over and kept slowly rotating.

"Unhand me, underling!" Keeper blustered. "I'll have you in irons. I'll tell Crown."

"Shooting weapons are as much against the law as knives or needles," Spar countered boldly, though he already was feeling dizzy and sick. "It's you should fear the brig." He recognized beneath the bullying voice the awe Keeper always had of his ability to move swiftly and surely, though half-blind.

They bounced to rest against a swarm of shrouds. "Loose me, I say," Keeper demanded, struggling weakly. "Crown gave me this pistol. And I have a permit for it from the Bridge." The last at least, Spar guessed, was a lie. Keeper continued, "Besides, it's only a line-shooting gun reworked for heavy, elastic ball. Not enough to rupture a wall, yet sufficient to knock out drunks—or knock in the head of a witch cat!"

"Not a witch cat, Keeper," Spar repeated, although he was having to swallow hard to keep from spewing. "Only a well-behaved stray, who has already proved his use to us by killing one of the rats that have been stealing our food. His name is Kim. He'll be a good worker."

The distant blur of Kim lengthened and showed thin blurs of legs and tail, as if he were standing out rampant from his line. "Assset izz I," he boasted. "Ssanitary. Uzze wasste tubes. Sslay ratss, micece! Sspy out witchchess, vampss ffor you!"

"He speaks!" Keeper gasped. "Witchcraft!"

149

"Crown has a dog who talks," Spar answered with finality. "A talking animal's no proof of anything."

All this while he had kept firm hold of barrel and finger. Now he felt through their grappled bodies a change in Keeper, as though inside his blubber the master of the Bat Rack were transforming from stocky muscle and bone into a very thick, sweet syrup that could conform to and flow around anything.

"Sorry, Spar," he whispered unctuously. "It was a bad night and Kim startled me. He's black like a witch cat. An easy mistake on my part. We'll try him out at catcher. he must earn his keep! Now take your drink."

The pliant double pouch filling Spar's palm felt like the philosopher's stone. He lifted it towards his lips, but at the same time his toes unwittingly found a shroud, and he dived swiftly towards the shining torus, which had a hole big enough to accommodate four barmen at a pinch.

Spar collapsed against the opposite inside of the hole. With a straining of its shrouds, the torus absorbed his impact. He had the pouch to his lips, its cap unscrewed, but had not squeezed. He shut his eyes and with a tiny sob blindly thrust the pouch back into the moonmist cage.

Working chiefly by touch, he took a pouch of corn gruel from the hot closet, snitching at the same time a pouch of coffee and thrusting it into an inside pocket. Then he took a pouch of water, opened it, shoved in five salt tablets, closed it, and shook and squeezed it vigorously.

Keeper, having drifted behind him, said into his ear, "So you drink anyhow. Moonmist not good enough, you make yourself a cocktail. I should dock it from your scrip. But all drunks are liars, or become so."

Unable to ignore the taunt, Spar explained, "No, only salt water to harden my gums."

150

"Poor Spar, what'll you ever need hard gums for? Planning to share rats with your new friend? Don't let me catch you roasting them in my grill! I should dock you for the salt. To sweeping, Spar!" Then turning his head towards the violet forecorner and speaking loudly, "And you! Catch mice!"

Kim had already found the small chewer tube and thrust the dead rat into it, gripping tube with foreclaws and pushing rat with aft. At the touch of the rat's cadaver against the solid wrist of the tube, a grinding began there which would continue until the rat was macerated and slowly swallowed away towards the great cloaca which fed the Gardens of Diana.

Three times Spar manfully swished salt water against his gums and spat into waste tube, vomiting a little after the first gargle. Then facing away from Keeper as he gently squeezed the pouches, he forced into his throat the coffee—dearer than moonmist, the drink distilled from moonbrew—and some of the corn gruel.

He apologetically offered the rest to Kim, who shook his head. "Jusst had a mousse."

Hastily Spar made his way to the green starboard corner. Outside the hatch he heard some drunks calling with weary and mournful anger, "Unzip!"

Grasping the heads of two long waste tubes, Spar began to sweep the air, working out from the green corner in a spiral, quite like an orb spider building her web.

From the torus, where he was idly polishing its thin titanium, Keeper upped the suction on the two tubes, so that reaction sped Spar in his spiral. He need use his body only to steer course and to avoid shrouds in such a way that his tubes didn't tangle.

Soon Keeper glanced at his wrist and called, "Spar, can't you keep track of the time? Open up!" He threw a ring of keys which Spar caught, though he could see only the last half of their flight. As soon as he was well headed towards the green door, Keeper called again and pointed aft and aloft. Spar obediently unlocked and unzipped the dark and also the blue hatch, though there was no one at either, before opening the green. In each case he avoided the hatch's gummy margin and the sticky emergency hatch hinged close beside.

In tumbled three brewos, old customers, snatching at shrouds and pushing off from each other's bodies in their haste to reach the torus, and meanwhile cursing Spar.

"Sky strangle you!"

"Earth bury you!"

"Seas sear you!"

"Language, boys!" Keeper reproved. "Though I'll agree my helper's stupidity and sloth tempt a man to talk foul."

Spar threw the keys back. The brewos lined up elbow to elbow around the torus, three greyish blobs with heads pointing towards the blue corner.

Keeper faced them. "Below, below!" he ordered indignantly. "You think you're gents?"

"But you're serving no one aloft yet."

"There's only us three."

"No matter," Keeper replied. "Propriety, suckers! Unless you mean to buy by the pouch, invert."

With low grumbles the brewos reversed their bodies so that their heads pointed towards the black corner.

Himself not bothering to invert, Keeper tossed them a slim and twisty faint red blur with three branches. Each grabbed a branch and stuck it in his face.

The pudge of his fat hand on glint of valve, Keeper said, "Let's see your scrip first."

With angry mumbles each unwadded something too small for Spar to see clearly, and handed it over. Keeper studied each item before feeding it to the cashbox. Then he

152

decreed, "Six seconds of moonbrew. Suck fast," and looked at his wrist and moved the other hand.

One of the brewos seemed to be strangling, but he blew out through his nose and kept sucking bravely.

Keeper closed the valve.

Instantly one brewo splutteringly accused, "You cut us off too soon. That wasn't six."

The treacle back in his voice, Keeper explained, "I'm squirting it to you four and two. Don't want you to drown. Ready again?"

The brewos greedily took their second squirt and then, at times wistfully sucking their tubes for remnant drops, began to shoot the breeze. In his distant circling, Spar's keen ears heard most of it.

"A dirty Sleepday, Keeper."

"No, a good one, brewo—for a drunken sucker to get his blood sucked by a lust-tickling vamp."

"I was dossed safe at Pete's, you fat ghoul."

"Pete's safe? That's news!"

"Dirty Atoms to you! But vamps did get Girlie and Sweetheart. Right in the starboard main drag, if you can believe it. By Cobalt Ninety, Windrush is getting lonely! Third Hold, anyhow. You can swim a whole passageway by day without meeting a soul."

"How do you know that about the girls?" the second brewo demanded. "Maybe they've gone to another hold to change their luck."

"Their luck's run out. Suzy saw them snatched."

"Not Suzy," Keeper corrected, now playing umpire. "But Mable did. A proper fate for drunken sluts."

"You've got no heart, Keeper."

"True enough. That's why the vamps pass me by. But speaking serious, boys, the werethings and witches are running too free in Three. I was awake all Sleepday guarding. I'm sending a complaint to the bridge."

"You're kidding."

"You wouldn't."

Keeper solemnly nodded his head and crossed his left chest. The brewos were impressed.

Spar spiralled back towards the green corner, sweeping farther from the wall. On his way he overtook the black blob of Kim, who was circling the periphery himself, industriously leaping from shroud to shroud and occasionally making dashes along them.

A fair-skinned, plump shape twice circled by blue—bra and culottes—swam in through the green hatch.

"Morning Spar," a soft voice greeted. "How's it going?"

"Fair and foul," Spar replied. The golden cloud of blonde hair floating loose touched his face. "I'm quitting moonmist, Suzy."

"Don't be too hard on yourself, Spar. Work a day, loaf a day, play a day, sleep a day—that way it's best."

"I know. Workday, Loafday, Playday, Sleepday. Ten days make a terranth, twelve terranths make a sunth, twelve sunths make a starth, and so on, to the end of time. With corrections, some tell me. I wish I knew what all those names mean."

"You're too serious. You should—Oh, a kitten! How darling!"

"Kitten shmitten!" the big-headed black blur hissed as it leapt past them. "Izzz cat. IZZZ Kim."

"Kim's our new catcher," Spar explained. "He's serious too."

"Quit wasting time on old Toothless Eyeless, Suzy," Keeper called, "and come all the way in."

As Suzy complied with a sigh, taking the easy route of the ratlines, her soft taper fingers brushed Spar's crumpled cheek. "Dear Spar . . ." she murmured. As her feet passed his face, there was jingle of her charm-anklet—all gold-washed hearts, Spar knew.

"Hear about Girlie and Sweetheart?" a brewo greeted ghoulishly. "How'd you like your carotid or outside iliac sliced, your—?"

"Shut up sucker!" Suzy wearily cut him off. "Gimme a drink, Keeper."

"Your tab's long, Suzy. How are you going to pay?"

"Don't play games, Keeper, please. Not in the morning, anyhow. You know all the answers especially to that one. For now, a pouch of moonbrew, dark. And a little quiet."

"Pouches are for ladies, Suzy. I'll serve you aloft, you got to meet your marks, but—"

There was a shrill snarl which swiftly mounted to a scream of rage. Just inside the aft hatch, a pale figure in vermilion culottes and bra—no, wider than that, jacket or short coat—was struggling madly, somersaulting and kicking.

Entering carelessly, likely too swiftly, the slim girl had got parts of herself and her clothes stuck to the hatch's inside margin and the emergency hatch.

Breaking loose by frantic main force while Spar dived towards her and the brewos shouted advice, she streaked towards the torus, jerking at the ratlines, black hair streaming behind her.

Coming up with a *bong* of hip against titanium, she grabbed together her vermilion—yes, clutch coat with one hand and thrust the other across the rocking bar.

Drifting in close behind, Spar heard her say, "Double pouch of moonmist, Keeper. Make it fast."

"The best of mornings to you, Rixende," Keeper greeted. "I would gladly serve you goldwater, except, well—" The fat arms spread "—Crown doesn't like his girls coming to the Bat Rack by themselves. Last time he gave me strict orders to—"

"What the smoke! It's on Crown's account I came here, to find something he lost. Meanwhile, moonmist. Double!" She pounded on the bar until reaction started her aloft, and she pulled back into place with Spar's unthanked help.

"Softly, softly, lady," Keeper gentled, the tiny brown blurs of his eyes vanishing with his grinning. "What if Crown comes in while you're squeezing?"

"He won't!" Rixende denied vehemently, though glancing past Spar quickly—black blur or pale face, black blur again. "He's got a new girl. I don't mean Phanette or Doucette, but a girl you've never seen. Name of Almodie. He'll be busy with the skinny bitch all morning. And now uncage that double moonmist, you dirty devil!"

"Softly, Rixie. All in good time. What is it Crown lost?"

"A little black bag. About so big." She extended her slender hand, fingers merged. "He lost it here last Playday night, or had it lifted."

"Hear that, Spar?" Keeper said.

"No little black bags," Spar said very quickly. "But you did leave your big orange one here last night, Rixende. I'll get it." He swung inside the torus.

"Oh, damn both bags. Gimme that double!" the black-haired girl demanded frantically. "Earth Mother!"

Even the brewos gasped. Touching hands to the sides of his head, Keeper begged. "No big obscenities, please. They sound worse from a dainty girl, gentle Rixende."

"Earth Mother, I said! Now cut the fancy, Keeper, and give, before I scratch your face off and rummage your cages!"

"Very well, very well. At once, at once. But how will you pay? Crown told me he'd get my licence revoked if I ever put you on his tab again. Have you scrip? Or . . . coins?"

"Use your eyes! Or you think this coat's got inside pockets?" She spread it wide, flashing her upper body, then clutched it tight again. "Earth Mother! Earth Mother! Earth Mother!" The brewos babbled scandalized. Suzy snorted mildly in boredom.

With one fat hand-blob Keeper touched Rixende's wrist where a yellow blur circled it closely. "You've got gold," he said in hushed tones, his eyes vanishing again, this time in greed.

"You know damn well they're welded on. My anklets too."

"But these?" His hand went to a golden blur close beside her head.

"Welded too. Crown had my ears pierced."

"But . . ."

"Oh, you atom-dirty devil! I get you, all right. Well, then, *all right!*" The last words ended in a scream more of anger than pain as she grabbed a gold blur and jerked. Blood swiftly blobbed out. She thrust forward her fisted hand. "Now *give!* Gold for a double moonmist."

Keeper breathed hard but said nothing as he scrabbled in the moonmist cage, as if knowing he had gone too far. The brewos were silent too. Suzy sounded completely unimpressed as she said, *"And* my dark." Spar found a fresh dry sponge and expertly caught up the floating scarlet blobs with it before pressing it to Rixende's torn ear.

Keeper studied the heavy gold pendant, which he held close to his face. Rixende milked the double pouch pressed to her lips and her eyes vanished as she sucked blissfully. Spar guided Rixende's free hand to the sponge, and she automatically took over the task of holding it to her ear. Suzy gave a hopeless sigh, then reached her whole plump body across the bar, dipped her hand into a cool cage, and helped herself to a double of dark.

A long, wiry, very dark brown figure in skintight dark violet jumpers mottled with silver arrowed in from the dark red hatch at a speed half again as great as Spar ever dared and without brushing a single shroud by accident or intent. Midway the newcomer did a half somersault as he passed Spar, his long, narrow bare feet hit the titanium next to Rixende. He accordioned up so expertly that the torus hardly swayed.

One very dark brown arm snaked around her. The other plucked the pouch from her mouth, and there was a snap as he spun the cap shut.

A lazy musical voice inquired, "What'd we tell you would happen, baby, if you ever again took a drink on your own?"

The Bat Rack held very still. Keeper was backed against the opposite side of the hole, one hand behind him. Spar had his arm in his lost-and-found nook behind the moonbrew and the moonmist cages and kept it there. He felt fear-sweat beading on him. Suzy kept her dark close to her face.

A brewo burst into violent coughing, choked it to a wheezing end, and gasped subserviently, "Excuse me, coroner. Salutations."

Keeper chimed dully, "Morning . . . Crown."

Crown gently pulled the clutch coat off Rixende's fat shoulder and began to stroke her. "Why, you're all gooseflesh honey, and rigid as a corpse. What frightened you? Smooth down, skin. Ease up, muscles. Relax, Rix, and we'll give you a squirt."

His hand found the sponge, stopped, investigated, found the wet part, then went towards the middle of his face. He sniffed.

"Well, boys, at least we know none of you are vamps," he observed softly. "Else we'd found you sucking at her ear."

Rixende said very rapidly in a monotone, "I didn't come for a drink, I swear to you. I came to get that little bag you lost. Then I was tempted. I didn't know I would be. I tried to resist, but Keeper led me on. I—"

"Shut up," Crown said quietly. "We were just wondering how you paid him. Now we know. How were you planning to buy your third double? Cut off a hand or a foot? Keeper . . . show me your other hand. We said show it. That's right. Now unfist."

Crown plucked the pendant from Keeper's opened hand-blob. His yellow-brown eye-blurs on Keeper all the while, he wagged the precious bauble back and forth, then tossed it slowly aloft.

As the golden blur moved towards the open blue hatch at unchanging pace, Keeper opened and shut his mouth twice then babbled, "I didn't tempt her, Crown, honest I didn't. I didn't know she was going to hurt her ear. I tried to stop her but—"

"We're not interested," Crown said. "Put the double on our tab." His face never leaving Keeper's he extended his arm aloft and pinched the pendant just before it straight-lined out of reach.

"Why's this home of jollity so dead?" Snaking a long leg across the bar as easily as an arm, Crown pinched Spar's ear betweeen his big and smaller toes, pulled him close and turned him round. "How're you coming along with the saline, baby? Gums hardening? Only one way to test it." Gripping Spar's jaw and lip with his other toes, he thrust the big one into Spar's mouth. "Come on, bite me, baby."

Spar bit. It was the only way not to vomit. Crown chuckled. Spar bit hard. Energy flooded his shaking frame. His face grew hot and his forehead throbbed under its drenching of fear-sweat. He was sure he was hurting Crown, but the Coroner of Hold Three only kept up his low, delighted chuckle and when Spar gasped, withdrew his foot.

"My, my, you're getting strong, baby. We almost felt that. Have a drink on us."

Spar ducked his stupidly wide-open mouth away from the thin jet of moonmist. The jet struck him in his eye and stung so that he had to knock his fists and clamp his aching gums together to keep from crying out.

"Why's this place so dead, I ask again? No applause for baby and now baby's gone temperance on us. Can't you give us just one tiny laugh?" Crown faced each in turn. "What's the matter? Cat got your tongues?"

"Cat? We have a cat, a new cat, came just last night, working as catcher," Keeper suddenly babbled. "It can talk a little. Not as well as Hellhound, but it talks. It's very funny. It caught a rat."

"What'd you do with the rat's body, Keeper?"

"Fed it to the chewer. That is Spar did. Or the cat."

"You mean to tell us that you disposed of a corpse without notifying us? Oh, don't go pale on us, Keeper. That's nothing. Why, we could accuse you of harbouring a witch cat. You say he came last night, and that was a wicked night for witches. Now don't go green on us too. We were only putting you on. We were only looking for a small laugh."

"Spar! Call your cat! Make him say something funny."

Before Spar could call, or even decide whether he'd call Kim or not, the black blur appeared on a shroud near Crown, green eye-blurs fixed on the yellow-brown ones.

"So you're the joker, eh? Well . . . joke."

Kim increased in size. Spar realized it was his fur standing on end.

"Go ahead, joke . . . like they tell us you can. Keeper, you wouldn't be kidding us about this cat being able to talk?"

160

"Spar! Make your cat joke!"

"Don't bother. We believe he's got his own tongue too. That the matter, Blackie?" He reached out his hand. Kim lashed at it and sprang away. Crown only gave another of his low chuckles.

Rixende began to shake uncontrollably. Crown examined her solicitously yet leisurely, using his outstretched hand to turn her head towards him, so that any blood that might have been coming from it from the cat's slash would have gone into the sponge.

"Spar swore the cat could talk," Keeper babbled. "I'll—"

"Quiet," Crown said. He put the pouch to Rixende's lips, squeezed until her shaking subsided and it was empty, then flicked the crumpled pliofilm towards Spar.

"And now about that little black bag, Keeper," Crown said flatly.

"Spar!"

That latter dipped into his lost-and-found nook, saying quickly, "No little black bags, coroner, but we did find this one the lady Rixende forgot last Playday night," and he turned back holding out something big, round, gleamingly orange, and closed with drawstrings.

Crown took and swung it slowly in a circle. For Spar, who couldn't see the strings, it was like magic. "Bit too big, and a mite the wrong shade. We're certain we lost the little black bag here, or had it lifted. You making the Bat Rack a tent for dips, Keeper?"

"Spar—?"

"We're asking *you*, Keeper."

Shoving Spar aside, Keeper groped frantically in the nook, pulling aside the cages of moonmist and moonbrew pouches. He produced many small objects. Spar could distinguish the largest—an electric hand-fan and a bright red foot-

161

glove. They hung around Keeper in a jumble.

Keeper was panting and had scrabbled his hands for a full minute in the nook without bringing out anything more, when Crown said, his voice lazy again, "That's enough. The little black bag was of no importance to us in any case."

Keeper emerged with a face doubly blurred. It must be surrounded by a haze of sweat. He pointed an arm at the orange bag.

"It must be inside that one!"

Crown opened the bag, began to search through it, changed his mind, and gave the whole bag a flick. Its remarkably numerous contents came out and moved slowly aloft at equal speeds, like an army on the march in irregular order. Crown scanned them as they went past.

"No, not there." He pushed the bag towards Keeper. "Return Rix's stuff to it and have it ready for us the next time we dive in—"

Putting his arm around Rixende, so that it was his hand that held the sponge to her ear, he turned and kicked off powerfully for the aft hatch. After he had been out of sight for several seconds, there was a general sigh, the three brewos put out new scrip-wads to pay for another squirt. Suzy asked for a second double dark, which Spar handed her quickly, while Keeper shook off his daze and ordered Spar, "Gather up all the floating trash, especially Rixie's, and get that back in her purse. On the jump, lubber!" Then he used the electric hand-fan to cool and dry himself.

It was a mean task Keeper had set Spar, but Kim came to help, darting after objects too small for Spar to see. Once he had them in his hands, Spar could readily finger or sniff which was which.

When his impotent rage at Crown had faded, Spar's thought went back to Sleepday night. Had his vision of vamps

162

and werewolves been dream only?—now that he knew the werethings had been abroad in force. If only he had better eyes to distinguish illusion from reality! Kim's "Sssee! Sssee shshsharply!" hissed in his memory. What would it be like to see sharply? Everything brighter? Or closer?

After a weary time the scattered objects were gathered and he went back to sweeping and Kim to his mouse hunt. As Workday morning progressed, the Bat Rack gradually grew less bright, though so gradually, it was hard to tell.

A few more customers came in, but all for quick drinks, which Keeper served them glumly; Suzy judged none of them worth cottoning up to.

As time slowly passed, Keeper grew steadily more fretfully angry, as Spar had known he would after grovelling before Crown. He tried to throw out the three brewos, but they produced more crumpled scrip, which closest scrutiny couldn't prove counterfeit. In revenge he short-squirted them and there were arguments. He called Spar off his sweeping to ask him nervously, "That cat of yours—he scratched Crown, didn't he? We'll have to get rid of him; Crown said he might be a witch cat, remember?" Spar made no answer. Keeper set him renewing the glue of the emergency hatches, claiming that Rixende's tearing free from the aft one had shown it must be drying out. He gobbled appetizers and drank moonmist with tomato juice. He sprayed the Bat Rack with some abominable synthetic scent. He started counting the boxed scrip and coins but gave up the job with a slam of self-locking drawer almost before he'd begun. His grimace fixed on Suzy.

"Spar!" he called. "Take over! And over-squirt the brewos on your peril!"

Then he locked the cash box, and giving Suzy a meaningful jerk of his head towards the scarlet starboard hatch, he pulled himself towards it. With an unhappy shrug towards

Spar, she wearily followed.

As soon as the pair were gone, Spar gave the brewos an eight-second squirt, waving back their scrip, and placed two small serving cages—of fritos and yeast balls—before them. They grunted their thanks and fell to. The light changed from healthy bright to corpse white. There was a faint, distant roar, followed some seconds later by a brief crescendo of creakings. The new light made Spar uneasy. He served two more suck-and-dives and sold a pouch of moonmist at double purser's price. He started to eat an appetizer, but just then Kim swam in to show him proudly a mouse. He conquered his nausea, but began to dread the onset of real withdrawal symptoms.

A pot-bellied figure clad in sober black dragged itself along the ratlines from the green hatch. On the aloft side of the bar there appeared a visage in which the blur of white hair and beard almost hid leather-brown flesh, though accentuating the blurs of grey eyes.

"Doc!" Spar greeted, his misery and unease gone, and instantly handed out a chill pouch of three-star moonbrew. Yet all he could think to say in his excitement was the banal, "A bad Sleepday night, eh, Doc? Vamps and—"

"—And other doltish superstitions, which wax every sunth, but never wane," an amiable, cynical old voice cut in. "Yet I suppose I shouldn't rob you of your illusions, Spar, even the terrifying ones. You've little enough to live by, as it is. And there *is* viciousness astir in Windrush. Ah, that smacks good against my tonsils."

The Spar remembered the important thing. Reaching deep inside his slopsuit, he brought out, in such a way as to hide it from the brewos below, a small flat narrow black bag.

"Here Doc," he whispered, "you lost it last Playday. I kept it safe for you."

"Dammit, I'd lose my jumpers, if I ever took them off,"

Doc commented, hushing his voice when Spar put finger to lips. "I suppose I started mixing moonmist with my moonbrew—again?"

"You did, Doc. But you didn't lose your bag. Crown or one of his girls lifted it, or snagged it when it sat loose beside you. And then I . . . I, Doc, lifted it from Crown's hip pocket. Yes, and kept that secret when Rixende and Crown came in demanding it this morning.

"Spar, my boy, I am deeply in your debt," Doc said. "More than you can know. Another three-star, please. Ah, nectar Spar, ask any reward of me, and if it lies merely within the realm of the first transfinite infinity, I will grant it."

To his own surprise, Spar began to shake—with excitement. Pulling himself forward halfway across the bar he whispered hoarsely, "Give me good eyes, Doc!" adding impulsively, "and teeth!"

After what seemed a long while, Doc said in a dreamy sorrowful voice, "In the Old Days, that would have been easy. They'd perfected eye transplants. They could regenerate cranial nerves, and sometimes restore scanning power to an injured cerebrum. While transplanting tooth buds from a stillborn was intern's play. But now . . . Oh, I might be able to do what you ask in an uncomfortable, antique, inorganic fashion, but . . ." He broke off on a note that spoke of the misery of life and the uselessness of all effort.

"These Old Days," one brewo said from the corner of his mouth to the brewo next to him. "Witch talk!"

"Witch-smitch!" the second brewo replied in like fashion. "The flesh mechanic's only senile. He dreams all four days, not just Sleepday."

The third brewo whistled against the evil eye a tune like the wind.

Spar tugged at the long-armed sleeve of Doc's black

jumper. "Doc, you promised. I want to see sharp, bite sharp!"

Doc laid his shrunken hand commiseratingly on Spar's forearm. "Spar," he said softly, "seeing sharply would only make you very unhappy. Believe me, I *know*. Life's easier to bear when things are blurred, just as it's best when thoughts are blurred by brew or mist. And while there are people in Windrush who yearn to bite sharply, you are not their kind. Another three-star, if you please.

"I quit moonmist this morning, Doc," Spar said somewhat proudly as he handed over the fresh pouch.

Doc answered with sad smile, "Many quit moonmist every Workday morning and change their minds when Playday comes around."

"Not me, Doc! Besides," Spar argued, "Keeper and Crown and his girls and even Suzy all see sharply, and they aren't unhappy."

"I'll tell you a secret, Spar," Doc replied. "Keeper and Crown and the girls are all zombies. Yes, even Crown with his cunning and power. To them Windrush is the universe."

"It isn't, Doc?"

Ignoring the interruption, Doc continued, "But you wouldn't be like that, Spar. You'd want to know more. And that would make you far unhappier than you are."

"I don't care, Doc," Spar said. He repeated accusingly, "You promised."

The grey blurs of Doc's eyes almost vanished as he frowned in thought. Then he said, "How would this be, Spar? I know moonmist brings pain and sufferings as well as easings and joys. But suppose that every Workday morning and Loafday noon I should bring you a tiny pill that would give you all the good effects of moonmist and none of the bad. I've one in this bag. Try it now and see. And every Playday night I would bring you without fail another sort of pill that would make you sleep soundly with never a nightmare. Much better than eyes and teeth. Think it over."

As Spar considered that, Kim drifted up. He eyed Doc with his close-set green blurs. "Resspectfful greetingss, ssir," he hissed. "Name izz Kim."

Doc answered, "The same to you, sir. May mice be ever abundant." He softly stroked the cat, beginning with Kim's chin and chest. The dreaminess returned to his voice. "In the Old Days, all cats talked, not just a few sports. The entire feline tribe. And many dogs, too—pardon me, Kim. While as for dolphins and whales and apes . . ."

Spar said eagerly, "Answer me one question, Doc. If your pills give happiness without hangover, why do you always drink moonbrew yourself and sometimes spike it with moonmist?"

"Because for me—" Doc began and then broke off with a grin. "You've trapped me, Spar. I never thought you used your mind. Very well, on your own mind be it. Come to my office this Loafday—you know the way? Good!—and we'll see what we can do about your eyes and teeth. And now a double pouch for the corridor."

He paid in bright coins, thrust the big squunchy three-star in a big pocket, said, "See you, Spar. So long, Kim," and tugged himself towards the green hatch, zig-zagging.

"Ffarewell, ssir," Kim hissed after him.

Spar held out the small black bag. "You forgot it again, Doc."

As Doc returned with a weary curse and pocketed it, the scarlet hatch unzipped and Keeper swam out. He looked in a good humor now and whistled the tune of "I'll Marry the Man on the Bridge" as he began to study certain rounds on scrip-till and moonbrew valves, but when Doc was gone he asked Spar suspiciously, "What was that you handed the old geezer?"

"His purse," Spar replied easily. "He forgot it now." He shook his loosely fisted hand and it chinked. "Doc paid in coins, Keeper." Keeper took them eagerly. "Back to sweeping, Spar."

As Spar dived towards the scarlet hatch to take up larboard tubes, Suzy emerged and passed him with face averted. She sidled up to the bar and unsmilingly snatched the pouch of moonmist Keeper offered her with mock courtliness.

Spar felt a brief rage on her behalf, but it was hard for him to keep his mind on anything but his coming appointment with Doc. When Workday night fell swiftly as a hurled knife, he was hardly aware of it and felt none of his customary unease. Keeper turned on full all of the lights in the Bat Rack. They shone brightly while beyond the translucent walls there was a milky churning.

Business picked up a little. Suzy made off with the first likely mark. Keeper called Spar to take over the torus, while he himself got a much-erased sheet of paper and holding it to a clipboard held against his bent knees, wrote on it laboriously, as if he were thinking out each word, perhaps each letter, often wetting his pencil in his mouth. He became so absorbed in his difficult task that without realizing he drifted off towards the black below hatch, rotating over and over. The paper got dirtier and dirtier with his scrawlings and smudgings, new erasures, saliva and sweat.

The short night passed more swiftly than Spar dared hope, so that the sudden glare of Loafday dawn startled him. Most of the customers made off to take their siestas.

Spar wondered what excuse to give Keeper for leaving the Bat Rack, but the problem was solved for him. Keeper folded the grimy sheet, and sealed it with hot tape. "Take this to the Bridge, loafer, to the Exec. Wait." He took the repacked, orange bag from its nook and pulled on the cords to make sure they were drawn tight. "On your way deliver this at Crown's Hole. With all courtesy and subservience, Spar! Now, on the jump!"

Spar slid the sealed message into his only pocket with working zipper and drew that tight. Then he dived slowly towards the aft hatch, where he almost collided with Kim. Recalling Keeper's talk of getting rid of the cat, he caught hold of him around the slim furry chest under the forelegs and gently thrust him inside his slopsuit, whispering, "You'll take a trip with me, little Kim." The cat set his claws in the thin material and steadied himself.

For spar, the corridor was a narrow cylinder ending in mist either way and decorated by lengthwise blurs of green and red. He guided himself chiefly by touch and memory, this time remembering that he must pull himself against the light wind hand-over-hand along the centerline. After curving past the larger cylinders of the fore-and-aft gangways, the corridor straightened. Twice he worked his way around centrally slung fans whirring so softly that he recognized them chiefly by the increase in breeze before passing them and the slight suction after.

Soon he began to smell oil and green stuff growing. With a shiver he passed a black round that was the elastic-curtained door to Hold Three's big chewer. He met no one— odd even for Loafday. Finally he saw the green of the Gardens of Apollo and beyond it a huge black screen, in which hovered towards the aft side a small, smokey-orange circle that always filled Spar with inexplicable sadness and fear. He wondered in how many black screens that doleful circle was portrayed, especially in the starboard end of Windrush. He had seen it in several.

So close to the gardens that he could make out wavering green shoots and the silhouette of a floating farmer, the corridor right-angled below. Two dozen pulls along the line and he floated by an open hatch, which both memory for distance and the strong scent of musky, mixed perfumes told him was the entry to Crown's Hole. Peering in, he could see the intermelting black and silver spirals of the decor of the great globular room. Directly opposite the hatch was another large black screen with red-mottled dun disc placed similarly off center.

From under Spar's chin, Kim hissed very softly, but urgently, "Sstop! Ssilencce, on your liffe!" The cat had poked his head out of the slopsuit's neck. His ears tickled Spar's throat. Spar was getting used to Kim's melodrama, and in any case the warning was hardly needed. He had just seen the half-dozen floating naked bodies and would have held still if only from embarrassment. Not that Spar could see genitals any more than ears at the distance. But he could see that save for hair, each body was of one texture: one very dark brown and the other—five or was it four? no five—fair. He didn't recognize the two with platinum and golden hair, who also happened to be the two palest. He wondered which was Crown's new girl, name of Almodie. He was relieved that none of the bodies were touching.

There was a glint of metal by the golden-haired girl, and he could just discern the red blur of a slender, five-forked tube which went from the metal to the five other faces. It seemed strange that even with a girl to play bartender, Crown should have moonbrew served in such plebeian fashion in his palatial Hole. Of course the tube might carry moonwine, or even moonmist.

Or was Crown planning to open a rival bar to the Bat Rack? A poor time, these days, and a worse location, he mused as he tried to think of what to do with the orange bag.

"Sslink offf!" Kim urged still more softly.

170

Spar's fingers found a snap-ring by the hatch. With the faintest of clicks he secured it around the draw-cords of the pouch and then pulled back the way he had come.

But faint as the click had been, there was a response from Crown's Hole—a very deep, long growl.

Spar pulled faster at the centerline. As he rounded the corner leading inboard, he looked back.

Jutting out from Crown's hatch was a big, prick-eared head narrower than a man's and darker even than Crown's.

The growl was repeated.

It was ridiculous he should be so frightened of Hellhound, Spar told himself as he jerked himself and his passenger along. Why, Crown sometimes even brought the big dog to the Bat Rack.

Perhaps it was the Hellhound never growled in the Bat Rack, only talked in a hundred or so monosyllables.

Besides, the dog couldn't pull himself along the centerline at any speed. He lacked sharp claws. Though he might be able to bound forward, caroming from one side of the corridor to another.

This time the center-slit black curtains of the big chewer made Spar veer violently. He was a fine one—going to get new eyes today and frightened as a child!

"Why did you try to scare me back there, Kim?" he asked angrily.

"I ssaw shsheer evil, isssiot!"

"You saw five folk sucking moonbrew. And a harmless dog. This time you're the fool, Kim, you're the idiot!"

Kim shut up, drawing in his head, and refused to say another word. Spar remembered about the vanity and touchiness of all cats. But by now he had other worries. What if the orange bag were stolen by a passerby before Crown noticed it? And if Crown did find it, wouldn't he know Spar, forever

171

Keeper's errand-boy, had been peering? That all this should happen on the most important day of his life!! His verbal victory over Kim was small consolation.

Also, although the platinum-haired girl had interested him most of the two strange ones, something began to bother him about the girl who'd been playing bartender, the one with golden hair like Suzy's, but much slimmer and paler—he had the feeling he'd seen her before. And something about her had frightened him.

When he reached the central gangways, he was tempted to go to Doc's office before the Bridge. But he wanted to be able to relax at Doc's and take as much time as needed, knowing all errands were done.

Reluctantly he entered the windy violet gangway and dived at a fore angle for the first empty space on the central gang-line, so that his palms were only burned a little before he had firm hold of it and was being sped fore at about the same speed as the wind. Keeper was a miser, not to buy him handgloves, let alone footgloves!—but he had to pay sharp attention to passing the shroud-slung roller bearings that kept the thick, moving line centerd in the big corridor. It was an easy trick to catch hold of the line ahead of the bearings and then get one's other hand out of the way, but it demanded watchfulness.

There were few figures travelling on the line and fewer still being blown along the corridor. He overtook a doubled up one tumbling over and over and crying out in an old cracked voice, "Jacob's Ladder, Tree of Life, Marriage Lines . . ."

He passed the squeeze in the gangway marking the division between the Third and Second Holds without being stopped by the guard there and then he almost missed the big blue corridor leading aloft. Again he slightly burned his palms making the transfer from one moving gang-line to another. His fretfulness increased.

"Sspar, you isssiot—?" Kim began.

"Ssh!—we're in officers' territory," Spar cut him off, glad to have that excuse for once more putting down the impudent cat. And true enough, the blue spaces of Windrush always did fill him with awe and dread.

Almost too soon to suit him, he found himself swinging from the gang-line to a stationary monkey jungle of tubular metal just below the deck of the Bridge. He worked his way to the aloftmost bars and floated there, waiting to be spoken to.

Much metal, in many strange shapes, gleamed in the Bridge, and there were irregularly pulsing rainbow surfaces, the closest of which sometimes seemed ranks and files of tiny lights going on and off—red, green, all colors. Aloft of everything was an endless velvet-black expanse very faintly blotched by churning, milky glintings.

Among the metal objects and the rainbows floated figures all clad in the midnight blue of officers. They sometimes gestured to each other, but never spoke a word. To Spar, each of their movements was freighted with profound significance. These were the gods of Windrush, who guided everything, if there were gods at all. He felt reduced in importance to a mouse, which would be chased off chittering if it once broke silence.

After a particularly tense flurry of gesture, there came a brief distant roar and a familiar creaking and crackling. Spar was amazed, yet at the same time realized he should have known that the Captain, the Navigator, and the rest were responsible for the familiar diurnal phenomena.

It also marked Loafday noon. Spar began to fret. His errands were taking too long. He began to lift his hand tenta-

tively towards each passing figure in midnight blue. None took the least note of him.

Finally he whispered, "Kim—?"

The cat did not reply. He could hear a purring that might be a snore. He gently shook the cat. "Kim, let's talk."

"Shshut offf! I ssleep! Ssh!" Kim resettled himself and his claws and recommenced his purring snore—whether natural or feigned, Spar could not tell. He felt very despondent.

The lunths crept by. He grew desperate and weary. He must not miss his appointment with Doc! He was nerving himself to move farther aloft and speak, when he heard a pleasant "Hello, grandpa, what's on your mind?"

Spar realized that he had been raising his hand automatically and that a person as dark-skinned as Crown, but clad in midnight blue, had at last taken notice. He unzipped the note and handed it over. "For the Exec."

"That's my department." A trilled crackle—fingernail slitting the note? A larger crackle—note being opened. A brief wait. Then, "Who's Keeper?"

"Owner of the Bat Rack, sir. I work there."

"Bat Rack?"

"A moonbrew mansion. Once called the Happy Torus, I've been told. In the Old Days, Wine Mess Three, Doc told me."

"Hmmmm. Well, what's all this mean, gramps? And what's your name?"

Spar stared miserably at the dark-mottled grey square. "I can't read, sir. Name's Spar."

"Hmmm. Seen any . . . er . . . supernatural beings in the Bat Rack?"

"Only in my dreams, sir."

"Mmmm. Well, we'll have a look in. If you recognize me, don't let on. I'm Ensign Drake, by the way. Who's your passenger, grandpa?"

"Only my cat, Ensign," Spar breathed in alarm.

"Well, take the black shaft down." Spar began to move across the monkey jungle in the direction pointed out by the blue arm-blur.

"And next time remember animals aren't allowed on the Bridge."

As Spar travelled below, his warm relief that Ensign Drake had seemed quite human and compassionate was mixed with anxiety as to whether he still had time to visit Doc. He almost missed the shift to the gang-line grinding aft in the dark red main-drag. The corpse light brightening into the false dawn of late afternoon bothered him. Once more he passed the tumbling bent figure, this time croaking, "Trinity, Trellis, Wheat Ear . . ."

He was fighting down the urge to give up his visit to Doc and pull home to the Bat Rack, when he noticed he had passed the second squeeze and was in Hold Four with the passageway to Doc's coming up. He dived off, checked himself on a shroud and began the hand-drag to Doc's office, as far larboard as Crown's Hole was starboard.

He passed two figures clumsy on the line, their breaths malty in anticipation of Playday. Spar worried that Doc might have closed his office. He smelled soil and greenery again, from the Gardens of Diana.

The hatch was shut, but when Spar pressed the bulb, it unzipped after three honks, and the white-haloed grey-eyed face peered out.

"I'd just about given up on you, Spar."

"I'm sorry, Doc. I had to—"

"No matter. Come in, come in, Hello, Kim—take a look around if you want."

Kim crawled out, pushed off from Spar's chest, and

soon was engaged in a typical cat's tour of inspection.

And there was a great deal to inspect, as even Spar could see. Every shroud in Doc's office seemed to have objects clipped along its entire length. There were blobs large and small, gleaming and dull, light and dark, translucent and solid. They were silhouetted against a wall of the corpse-light Spar feared, but had no time to think of now. At one end was a band of even brighter light.

"Careful, Kim!" Spar called to the cat as he landed against a shroud and began to paw his way from blob to blob.

"He's all right," Doc said. "Let's have a look at you, Spar. Keep your eyes open."

Doc's hands held Spar's head. The grey eyes and leathery face came so close they were one blur.

"Keep them open, I said. Yes, I know you have to blink them, that's all right. Just as I thought. The lenses are dissolved. You've suffered the side-effect which one in ten do who are infected with the Lethean rickettsia."

"Styx ricks, Doc?"

"That's right, though the mob's got hold of the wrong river in the Underworld. But we've all had it. We've all drunk the water of Lethe. Though sometimes when we grow very old we begin to remember the beginning. Don't squirm."

"Hey, Doc, is it because I've had the Styx ricks I can't remember anything back before the Bat Rack?"

"It could be. How long have you been at the Rack?"

"I don't know, Doc. Forever."

"Before I found the place, anyhow. Then the Rumdum closed here in Four. But that's only a starth ago."

"But I'm awful old, Doc. Why don't I start remembering?"

"You're not old, Spar. You're just bald and toothless and etched by moonist and your muscles have shrivelled. Yes, and

178

your mind has shrivelled too. Now open your mouth."

One of Doc's hands went to the back of Spar's neck. The other probed. "Your gums are tough, anyhow. That'll make it easier."

Spar wanted to tell about the salt water, but when Doc finally took his hand out of Spar's mouth, it was to say, "Now open wide as you can."

Doc pushed into his mouth something big as a handbag and hot. "Now bite down hard."

Spar felt as if he had bitten fire. He tried to open his mouth, but hands on his head and jaw held it closed. Involuntarily he kicked and clawed air. His eyes filled with tears.

"Stop writhing! Breathe through your nose. It's not that hot. Not hot enough to blister, anyhow."

Spar doubted that, but after a bit decided it wasn't quite hot enough to bake his brain through the roof of his mouth. Besides he didn't want to show Doc his cowardice. He held still. He blinked several times and the general blur became the blurs of Doc's face and the cluttered room silhouetted by the corpse-glare. He tried to smile, but his lips were already stretched wider than their muscles could ever have done. That hurt too; he realized now that the heat was abating a little.

Doc was grinning for him. "Well, you would ask an old drunkard to use techniques he'd only read about. To make it up to you, I'll give you teeth sharp enough to sever shrouds. Kim, please get away from that bag.

The black blur of the cat was pushing off from a black blur twice his length. Spar mumbled disapprovingly at Kim through his nose and made motions. The larger blur was shaped like Doc's little bag, but bigger than a hundred of them. It must be massive too, for in reaction to Kim's push it had bent the shroud to which it was attached and—the

179

point—the shroud was very slow in straightening.

"That bag contains my treasure, Spar," Doc explained, and when Spar lifted his eyebrows twice to signal another question, went on, "No, not coin and gold and jewels, but a second transfinite infinitude—sleep and dreams and nightmares for every soul in a thousand Windrushes." He glanced at his wrist. "Time enough now. Open your mouth." Spar obeyed, though it cost him new pain.

Doc withdrew what Spar had bitten on, wrapped it in gleam, and clipped it to the nearest shroud. Then he looked in Spar's mouth again.

"I guess I did make it a bit too hot," he said. He found a small pouch, set it to Spar's lips, and squeezed it. A mist filled Spar's mouth and all pain vanished.

Doc tucked the pouch in Spar's pocket. "If the pain returns, use it again."

But before Spar could thank Doc, the latter had pressed a tube to his eye. "Look, Spar, what do you see?"

Spar cried out, he couldn't help it, and jerked his eye away.

"What's wrong, Spar?"

"Doc, you gave me a dream," Spar said hoarsely. "You won't tell anyone, will you? And it tickled."

"What was the dream like?" Doc asked eagerly.

"Just a picture, Doc. The picture of a goat with the tail of a fish. Doc, I saw the fish's . . ." His mind groped, ". . . scales! Everything had . . . edges! Doc, is *that* what they mean when they talk about seeing sharply?"

"Of course, Spar. This is good. It means there's no cerebral or retinal damage. I'll have no trouble making up field glasses—that is, if there's nothing seriously wrong with my antique pair. So you still see things sharp-edged in dreams—that's natural enough. But why were you afraid of telling?"

180

"Afraid of being accused of witchcraft, Doc. I thought seeing things like that was clairvoyance. The tube tickled my eye a little."

"Isotopes and insanity! It's supposed to tickle. Let's try the other eye."

Again Spar wanted to cry out, but he restrained himself, and this time he had no impulse to jerk his eye away, although there was again the faint tickling. The picture was that of a slim girl. He could tell she was female because of her general shape. But he could see her edges. He could see . . . details. For instance, her eyes weren't mist-bounded colored ovals. They had points at both ends, which were china-white . . . triangles. And the pale violet round between the triangles had a tiny black round at its center.

She had silvery hair, yet she looked young, he thought, though it was hard to judge such matter when you could see edges. She made him think of the platinum-haired girl he'd glimpsed in Crown's Hole.

She wore a long, gleaming white dress, which left her shoulders bare, but either art or some unknown force had drawn her hair and her dress towards her feet. In her dress it made . . . folds.

"What's her name Doc? Almodie?"

"No. Virgo. The Virgin. You can see her edges?"

"Yes, Doc. Sharp. I get it!—like a knife. And the goat-fish?"

"Capricorn," Doc answered, removing the tube from Spar's eye.

"Doc, I know Capricorn and Virgo are the names of lunths, terranths, sunths, and starths, but I never knew they had pictures. I never knew they *were* anything."

"You—Of course, you've never seen watches, or stars, let alone the constellations of the zodiac."

181

Spar was about to ask what all *those* were, but then he saw that the corpse-light was all gone, although the ribbon of brighter light had grown very wide.

"At least in this stretch of your memory," Doc added. "I should have your new eyes and teeth ready next Loafday. Come earlier if you can manage. I may see you before that at the Bat Rack, Playday night or earlier."

"Great, Doc, but now I've got to haul. Come on, Kim. Sometimes business heavies up Loafday night, Doc, like it was Playday night come at the wrong end. Jump in, Kim."

"Sure you can make it back to the Bat Rack all right, Spar? It'll be dark before you get there."

"Course I can, Doc."

But when night fell, like a heavy hood jerked down over his head, halfway down the first passageway, he would have gone back to ask Doc to guide him except he feared Kim's contempt, even though the cat still wasn't talking. He pulled ahead rapidly, though the few running lights hardly let him see the centerline.

The fore gangway was even worse—completely empty and its lights dim and flickering. Seeing blurs bothered him now that he knew what seeing sharp was like. He was beginning to sweat and shake and cramp from his withdrawal from alcohol and his thoughts were a tumult. He wondered if *any* of the weird things that had happened since meeting Kim were real or dream. Kim's refusal—or inability?—to talk any more was disquieting. He began seeing the misty rims of blurs that vanished when he looked straight towards them. He remembered Keeper and the brewos talking about vamps and witches.

Then instead of waiting for the Bat Rack's green hatch, he dived off into the passageway leading to the aft one. This passageway had no lights at all. Out of it he thought he could hear Hellhound growling, but couldn't be sure because the big chewer was grinding. He was scrabbling with panic when he entered the Bat Rack through the dark red hatch, remembering barely in time to avoid the new glue.

The place was jumping with light and excitement and dancing figures, and Keeper at once began to shout abuse at him. He dived into the torus and began taking orders and serving automatically, working entirely by touch and voice, because withdrawal now had his vision swimming—a spinning blur of blurs.

After a while that got better, but his nerves got worse. Only the unceasing work kept him going—and shut out Keeper's abuse—but he was getting too tired to work at all. As Playday dawned, with the crowd around the torus getting thicker all the while, he snatched a pouch of moonmist and set it to his lips.

Claws dug his chest. "Isssiot! Sssot! Ssslave of fffear!"

Spar almost went into convulsions, but put back the moonmist. Kim came out of the slopsuit and pushed off contemptuously, circled the bar and talked to various of the drinkers, soon became a conversation piece. Keeper started to boast about him and quit serving. Spar worked on and on and on through sobriety more nightmarish than any drunk he could recall. And far, far longer.

Suzy came in with a mark and touched Spar's hand when he served her dark to her. It helped.

He thought he recognized a voice from below. It came from a kinky-haired, slopsuited brewo he didn't know. But then he heard the man again and thought he was Ensign Drake. There were several brewos he didn't recognize.

The place started really jumping. Keeper upped the music. Singly or in pairs, somersaulting dancers bounded back and forth between shrouds. Others toed a shroud and shim-

183

mied. A girl in black did splits on one. A girl in white dived through the torus. Keeper put it on her boyfriend's check. Brewos tried to sing.

Spar heard Kim recite:

"Izz a cat.
Killzz a rat.
Grreetss each guy,
Thin or ffat.
Saay dolls, hi!"

Playday night fell. The pace got hotter. Doc didn't come. But Crown did. Dancers parted and a whole section of drinkers made way aloft for him and his girls and Hellhound so that they had a third of the torus to themselves, with no one below in that third either. To Spar's surprise they all took coffee except the dog, who when asked by Crown, responded, "Bloody Mary," drawing out the words in such deep tones that they were little more than a low "Bluh-Muh" growl.

"Iss that sspeech, I assk you?" Kim commented from the other side of the torus. Drunks around him choked down chuckles.

Spar served the pouched coffee piping hot with felt holders and mixed Hellhound's drink in a self-squeezing syringe with sipping tube. He was very groggy and for the moment more afraid for Kim than himself. The face blurs tended to swim, but he could distinguish Rixende by her black hair, Phanette and Doucette by their matching red-blonde hair and oddly red-mottled fair skins, while Almodie *was* the platinum-haired one, yet she looked horribly right between the dark brown, purple-vested blur to one side of her and the blacked, narrower, prick-eared silhouette to the other.

Spar heard Crown whisper to her, "Ask Keeper to show

you the talking cat." The whisper was very low and Spar wouldn't have heard it except that Crown's voice had a strange excited vibrancy Spar had never known in it before.

"But won't they fight then?—I mean Hellhound," she answered in a voice that sent silver tendrils around Spar's heart. He yearned to see her face through Doc's tube. She would look like Virgo, only more beautiful. Yet, Crown's girl, she could be no virgin. It was a strange and horrible world. Her eyes *were* violet. But he was sick of blurs. Almodie sounded very frightened, yet she continued, "Please don't, Crown." Spar's heart was captured.

"But that's the whole idea, baby. And nobody don'ts us. We thought we'd schooled you to that. We'd teach you another lesson here, except tonight we smell his fuzz—lots of it, Keeper!—our new lady wishes to hear your cat talk. Bring it over."

"I really don't . . ." Almodie began and went no further.

Kim came floating across the torus while Keeper was shouting in the opposite direction. The cat checked himself against a slender shroud and looked straight at Crown. "Yesss?"

"Keeper, shut that junk off." The music died abruptly. Voices rose, then died abruptly too. "Well, cat, talk."

"Shshall ssing insstead," Kim announced and began an eerie caterwauling that had a pattern but was not Spar's idea of music.

"It's an abstraction," Almodie breathed delightedly. "Listen, Crown, that was a diminished seventh."

"A demented third, I'd say," Phanette commented from the other side.

Crown signed them to be quiet.

Kim finished with a high trill. He slowly looked around at his baffled audience and then began to groom his shoulder.

185

Crown gripped a ridge of the torus with his left hand and said evenly, "Since you will not talk to us, will you talk to our dog?"

Kim stared at Hellhound sucking his Bloody Mary. His eyes widened, their pupils slitted, his lips writhed back from needlelike fans.

He hissed, "Schschweinhund!"

Hellhound launched himself, hind paws against the palm of Crown's left hand, which threw him forward towards the left, where Kim was dodging. But the cat switched directions, rebounding hindwards from the next shroud. The dog's white-jagged jaws snapped sideways a foot from their mark as his great-chested black body hurtled past.

Hellhound landed with four paws in the middle of a fat drunk, who puffed out his wind barely before his swallow, but the dog took off instantly on reverse course. Kim bounced back and forth between shrouds. This time hair flew when jaws snapped, but also a rigidly spread paw slashed.

Crown grabbed Hellhound by his studded collar, restraining him from another dive. He touched the dog below the eye and smelled his fingers. "That'll be enough, boy," he said. "Can't go around killing musical geniuses." His hand dropped from his nose to below the torus and came up loosely fisted. "Well, cat, you've talked with our dog. Have you a word for us?"

"Yesss!" Kim drifted to the shroud nearest Crown's face. Spar pushed off to grab him back, while Almodie gazed at Crown's fist and edged a hand towards it.

Kim loudly hissed, "Hellzzz ssspawn! Fffiend!"

Both Spar and Almodie were too late. From between two of Crown's fisted fingers a needle-stream jetted and struck Kim in the open mouth.

After what seemed to Spar a long time, his hand interrupted the stream. Its back burned acutely.

Kim seemed to collapse into himself, then launched himself away from Crown, towards the dark, open-jawed.

Crown said, "That's mace, an antique weapon like Greek fire, but well-known to our folks. The perfect answer to a witch cat."

Spar sprang at Crown, grappled his chest, tried to butt his jaw. They moved away from the torus at half the speed with which Spar had sprung.

Crown got his head aside. Spar closed his gums on Crown's throat. There was a *snick*. Spar felt wind on his bare back. Then a cold triangle pressed his flesh over his kidneys. Spar opened his jaws and floated limp. Crown chuckled.

A blue fuzz-glare, held by a brewo, made everyone in the Bat Rack look more corpse-like than larboard light. A voice commanded, "Okay, folks, break it up. Go home. We're closing the place."

Sleepday dawned, drowning the fuzz-glare. The cold triangle left Spar's back. There was another *snick*. Saying, "Bye-bye, baby," Crown pushed off through the white glare towards four women's faces and one dog's. Phanette's and Doucette's faintly red-mottled ones were close beside Hellhound's as if they might be holding his collar.

Spar sobbed and began to hunt for Kim. After a while Suzy came to help him. The Bat Rack emptied. Spar and Suzy cornered Kim. Spar grasped the cat around the chest. Kim's forelegs embraced his wrist, claws pricking. Spar got out the pouch Doc had given him and shoved its mouth between Kim's jaws. The claws dug deep. Taking no note of that, Spar gently sprayed. Gradually the claws came out and Kim relaxed. Spar hugged him gently. Suzy bound up Spar's wounded wrist.

Keeper came up followed by two brewos, one of them Ensign Drake, who said, "My partner and I will watch today

187

by the aft and starboard hatches." Beyond them the Bat Rack was empty.

Spar said, "Crown has a knife." Drake nodded.

Suzy touched Spar's hand and said, "Keeper, I want to stay here tonight. I'm scared."

Keeper said, "I can offer you a shroud."

Drake and his mate dived slowly toward their posts.

Suzy squeezed Spar's hand. He said, rather heavily, "I can offer you my shroud, Suzy."

Keeper laughed and after looking towards the Bridge men whispered, "I can offer you mine, which, unlike Spar, I own. And moonmist. Otherwise, the passageways."

Suzy sighed, paused then went off with him.

Spar miserably made his way to the fore corner. Had Suzy expected him to fight Keeper? The sad thing was that he no longer wanted her, except as a friend. He loved Crown's new girl. Which was sad too.

He was very tired. Even the thought of new eyes tomorrow didn't interest him. He clipped his ankle to a shroud and tied a rag over his eyes. He gently clasped Kim, who had not spoken. He was asleep at once.

He dreamed of Almodie. She looked like Virgo, even to the white dress. She held Kim, who looked sleek as polished black leather. She was coming towards him smiling. She kept coming without getting closer.

Much later—he thought—he woke in the grip of withdrawal. He sweat and shook, but those were minor. His nerves were jumping. Any moment, he was sure, they would twitch all his muscles into a stabbing spasm of sinew-snapping agony. His thoughts were moving so fast he could hardly begin to understand one in ten. It was like speeding through a curving, ill-lit passageway ten times faster than the main drag. If he touched a wall, he would forget even what little Spar knew, forget he was Spar. All around him black shrouds whipped in perpetual sine curves.

Kim was no longer by him. He tore the rag from his eyes. It was dark as before. Sleepday night. But his body stopped speeding and his thoughts slowed. His nerves still crackled, and he still saw the black snakes whipping, but he knew them for illusion. He even made out the dim glows of three running lights.

Then he saw two figures floating towards him. He could barely make out their eye-blurs, green in the smaller, violet in the other, whose face was spreadingly haloed by silvery glints. She was pale and whiteness floated around her. And instead of a smile, he could see the white horizontal blur of bared teeth. Kim's teeth too were bared.

Suddenly he remembered the golden-haired girl who he'd thought was playing bartender in Crown's Hole. She was Suzy's onetime friend Sweetheart, snatched last Sleepday by vamps.

He screamed, which in Spar was a hoarse, retching bellow, and scrabbled at his clipped ankle.

The figures vanished. Below, he thought.

Lights came on. Someone dived and shook Spar's shoulder. "What happened, gramps?"

Spar gibbered while he thought what to tell Drake. He loved Almodie and Kim. He said, "Had a nightmare. Vamps attacked me."

"Description?"

"An old lady and a . . . a . . . little dog."

The other officer dived in. "The black hatch is open."

Drake said, "Keeper told us that was always locked. Follow through, Fenner." As the other dived below, "You're sure this was a nightmare, gramps? A *little* dog? And an *old* woman?"

189

Spar said, "Yes," and Drake dived after his comrade, out through the black hatch.

Workday dawned. Spar felt sick and confused, but he set about his usual routine. He tried to talk to Kim, but the cat was as silent as yesterday afternoon. Keeper bullied and found many tasks—the place was a mess from Playday. Suzy got away quickly. She didn't want to talk about Sweetheart or anything else. Drake and Fenner didn't come back.

Spar swept and Kim patrolled, out of touch. In the afternoon Crown came in and talked with Keeper while Spar and Kim were out of earshot. They mightn't have been there for all notice Crown took of them.

Spar wondered about what he had seen last night. It might really have been a dream, he decided. He was no longer impressed by his memory-identification of Sweetheart. Stupid of him to have thought that Almodie and Kim, dream or reality, were vamps. Doc had said vamps were superstitions. But he didn't think much. He still had withdrawal symptoms, only less violent.

When Loafday dawned, Keeper gave Spar permission to leave the Bat Rack without his usual prying questions. Spar looked around for Kim, but couldn't see his black blob. Besides, he didn't really want to take the cat.

He went straight to Doc's office. The passageways weren't as lonely as last Loafday. For a third time he passed the bent figure croaking, "Seagull, Kestrel, Cathedral . . ."

Doc's hatch was unzipped, but Doc wasn't there. Spar waited a long while, uneasy in the corpse-light. It wasn't like Doc to leave his office unzipped and unattended. And he hadn't turned up at the Bat Rack last night, as he'd half promised.

Finally Spar began to look around. One of the first things he noticed was that the big black bag, which Doc had said contained his treasure, was missing.

Then he noticed that the gleaming pliofilm bag in which Doc had put the mould of Spar's gums, now held something different. He unclipped it from its shroud. There were two items in it.

He cut a finger on the first, which was half circle, half pink and half gleaming. He felt out its shape more cautiously then, ignoring the tiny red blobs welling from his fingers. It had irregular depressions in its pink top and bottom. He put it in his mouth. His gums mated with the depressions. He opened his mouth, then closed it, careful to keep his tongue back. There was a *snick* and a dull *click*. He had teeth!

His hands were shaking, not just from withdrawal, as he felt the second time.

It was two thick rounds joined by a short bar and with a thicker long bar ending in a semicircle going back from each.

He thrust a finger into one of the rounds. It tickled, just as the tube had tickled his eyes, only more intensely, almost painfully.

Hands shaking worse than ever, he fitted the contraption to his face. The semicircles went around his ears, the rounds circled his eyes, not closely enough to tickle.

He could see sharply! *Everything* had edges, even his spread-fingered hands and the . . . clot of blood on one finger. He cried out—a low, wondering wail—and scanned the office. At first the scores and dozens of sharp-edged objects, each as distinct as the pictures of Capricorn and Virgo had been, were too much for him. He closed his eyes.

When his breathing was a little evener and his shaking less, he opened them cautiously and began to inspect the objects clipped to the shrouds. Each one was a wonder. He didn't know the purpose of half of them. Some of them with which he was familiar by use of blurred sight startled him

191

greatly in their appearance—a comb, a brush, a book with pages (that infinitude of ranked black marks), a wrist watch, the tiny pictures around the circular margin of Capricorn and Virgo, and of the Bull and the Fishes, and so on, and the narrow bars radiating from the center and swinging swiftly or slowly or not at all—and pointing to the signs of the zodiac.

Before he knew it, he was at the corpse-glow wall. He faced it with a new courage, though it forced from his lips another wondering wail.

The corpse-glow didn't come from everywhere, though it took up the central quarter of his field of vision. His fingers touched taut, transparent pliofilm. What he saw beyond—a great way beyond, he began to think—was utter blackness with a great many tiny . . . points of bright light in it. Points were even harder to believe in than edges, he had to believe what he saw.

But centrally, looking much bigger than all the blackness, was a vast corpse-white round pocked with faint circles and scored by bright lines and mottled with slightly darker areas.

It didn't look as if it were wired for electricity, and it certainly didn't look afire. After a while Spar got the weird idea that its light was reflected from something much brighter *behind* Windrush.

It was infinitely strange to think of so much *space* around Windrush. Like thinking of a reality containing reality.

And if Windrush were between the hypothetical brighter light and the pocked white round, its shadow ought to be on the latter. Unless Windrush were almost infinitely small. Really these speculations were utterly too fantastic to deal with.

Yet could anything be too fantastic? Werewolves, witches, points, edges, size and space beyond any but the most insane belief.

When he had first looked at the corpse-white object, it had been round. And he had heard and felt creakings of Loafday noon, without being conscious of it at the time. But now the round had its fore edge evenly sliced off, so that it was lopsided. Spar wondered if the hypothetical incandescence behind Windrush were moving, or the white round rotating, or Windrush itself revolving around the white round. Such thoughts, especially the last, were dizzying almost beyond endurance.

He made for the open door, wondering if he should zip it behind him, decided not to. The passageway was another amazement, going off and off and off, and narrowing as it went. Its walls bore . . . arrows, the red pointing to larboard, the way from which he'd come, the green pointing starboard, the way he was going. The arrows were what he'd always seen as dash-shaped blurs. As he pulled himself along the strangely definite dragline, the passageway stayed the same diameter, all the way to the violet main drag.

He wanted to jerk himself as fast as the green arrows to the starboard end of Windrush to verify the hypothetical incandescence and see the details of the orange-dun round that always depressed him.

But he decided he ought first to report Doc's disappearance to the Bridge. He might find Drake there. And report the loss of Doc's treasure too, he reminded himself.

Passing faces fascinated him. Such a welter of noses and ears! He overtook the croaking, bent shape. It was that of an old woman whose nose almost met her chin. She was doing something twitchy with her fingers to two narrow sticks and a roll of slender, fuzzy line. He impulsively dived off the dragline and caught hold of her, whirling them around.

"What are you doing, grandma?" he asked.

193

She puffed with anger, "Knitting," she answered indignantly.

"What are the words you keep saying?"

"Names of knitting patterns," she replied, jerking loose from him and blowing on. "Sand Dunes, Lightning, Soldiers Marching . . ."

He started to swim for the dragline, then saw he was already at the blue shaft leading aloft. He grabbed hold of its speeding centerline, not minding the burn, and speeded to the Bridge.

When he got there, he saw there was a multitude of stars aloft. The oblong rainbows were all banks of multi-colored lights winking on and off. But the silent officers—they looked very old, their faces stared as if they were sleep-swimming, their gestured orders were mechanical, he wondered if they knew where Windrush was going—or anything at all, beyond the Bridge of Windrush.

A dark young officer with tightly curly hair floated to him. It wasn't until he spoke that Spar knew he was Ensign Drake.

"Hello, gramps. Say, you look younger. What are those things around your eyes?"

"Field glasses. They help me see sharp."

"But fieldglasses have tubes. They're a sort of binocular telescope."

Spar shrugged and told about the disappearance of Doc and his big, black treasure bag.

"But you say he drank a lot and he told you his treasures were dreams? Sounds like he was wacky and wandered off to do his drinking somewhere else."

"But Doc was a regular drinker. He always came to the Bat Rack."

"Well, I'll do what I can. Say, I've been pulled off the Bat

Rack investigation. I think that character Crown got at some-one higher up. The old ones are easy to get at—not so much greed as going by custom, taking the easiest course. Fenner and I never did find the old woman and the little dog, or any female and animal . . . or anything."

Spar told about Crown's earlier attempt to steal Doc's little black bag.

"So you think the two cases might be connected. Well, as I say, I'll do what I can."

Spar went back to the Bat Rack. It was very strange to see Keeper's face in details. It looked old and its pink target center was a big red nose criss-crossed by veins. His brown eyes were not so much curious as avid. He asked about the things around Spar's eyes. Spar decided it wouldn't be wise to tell Keeper about seeing sharply.

"They're a new kind of costume jewelery, Keeper. Blasted Earth, I don't have any hair on my head, ought to have something."

"Language, Spar! It's like a drunk to spend precious scrip on such a grotesque bauble."

Spar neither reminded Keeper that all the scrip he'd earned at the Bat Rack amounted to no more than a wad as big as his thumb-joint, nor that he'd quit drinking. Nor did he tell him about his teeth, but kept them hidden behind his lips.

Kim was nowhere in sight. Keeper shrugged. "Gone off somewhere. You know the way of strays, Spar."

Yes, thought Spar, this one's stayed put too long.

He kept being amazed that he could see *all* of the Bat Rack sharply. It was an octahedron criss-crossed by shrouds and made up of two pyramids put together square base to square base. The apexes of the pyramids were the violet fore and dark red aft corners. The four other corners were the

195

starboard green, the black below, the larboard scarlet, and the blue aloft, if you named them from aft in the way the hands of a watch move.

Suzy drifted in early Playday. Spar was shocked by her blowsy appearance and bloodshot eyes. But he was touched by her signs of affection and he felt the strong friendship between them. Twice when Keeper wasn't looking he switched her nearly empty pouch of dark for a full one. She told him that, yes, she'd once known Sweetheart and that, yes, she'd heard people say Mable had seen Sweetheart snatched by vamps.

Business was slow for Playday. There were no strange brewos. Hoping against fearful, gut-level certainty, Spar kept waiting for Doc to come in zig-zagging along the ratlines and comment on the new gadgets he'd given Spar and spout about the Old Days and his strange philosophy.

Playday night Crown came in with his girls, all except Almodie. Doucette said she'd had a headache and stayed at the Hole. Once again, all of them ordered coffee, though to Spar all of them seemed high.

Spar covertly studied their faces. Though nervous and alive, they all had something in their stares akin to those he'd seen in most of the officers on the Bridge. Doc had said they were all zombies. It was interesting to find out that Phanette's and Doucette's red-mottled appearance was due to . . . freckles, tiny reddish star-clusters on their white skins.

"Where's that famous talking cat?" Crown asked Spar.

Spar shrugged. Keeper said, "Strayed. For which I'm glad. Don't want a little feline who makes fights like last night."

Keeping his yellow-brown irised eyes on Spar, Crown said, "We believe it was that fight last Playday gave Almodie her headache, so she didn't want to come back tonight. We'll tell her you got rid of the witch cat."

"I'd have got rid of the beast if Spar hadn't," Keeper put in. "So you think it was a witch cat, coroner?"

"We're certain. What's that stuff on Spar's face?"

"A new sort of cheap eye-jewelry, coroner, such as attracts drinks."

Spar got the feeling that this conversation had been pre-arranged, that there was a new agreement between Crown and Keeper. But he just shrugged again. Suzy was looking angry, but she said nothing.

Yet she stayed behind again after the Bat Rack closed. Keeper put no claim on her, though he leered knowlingly before disappearing with a yawn and a stretch through the scarlet hatch. Spar checked that all six hatches were locked and shut off the lights, though that made no difference in the morning glare, before returning to Suzy, who had gone to his sleeping shroud.

Suzy asked, "You didn't get rid of Kim?"

Spar answered, "No, he just strayed, as Keeper said at first. I don't know where Kim is."

Suzy smiled and put her arms around him. "I think your new eye-things are beautiful," she said.

Spar said, "Suzy, did you know that Windrush isn't the Universe? That it's a ship going through space around a white round marked with circles, a round much bigger than all Windrush?"

Suzy replied, "I know Windrush is sometimes called the Ship. I've seen that round—in pictures. Forget all wild thoughts, Spar, and lose yourself in me."

Spar did so, chiefly from friendship. He forgot to clip his ankle to the shroud. Suzy's body didn't attract him. He was thinking of Almodie.

When it was over, Suzy slept. Spar put the rag around his eyes and tried to do the same. He was troubled by withdrawal symptoms only a little less bad than last Sleepday's. Because of that little, he didn't go to the torus for a pouch of moonmist. But then there was a sharp jab in his back, as if a muscle had spasmed there, and the symptoms got much worse. He convulsed, once, twice, then just as the agony became unbearable, blanked out.

Spar woke, his head throbbing, to discover that he was not only clipped, but lashed to his shroud, his wrists stretched in one direction, his ankles in the other, his hands and his feet both numb. His nose rubbed the shroud.

Light made his eyelids red. He opened them a little at a time and saw Hellhound poised with bent hind legs against the next shroud. He could see Hellhound's great stabbing teeth very clearly. If he had opened his eyes a little more swiftly, Hellhound would have dived at his throat.

He rubbed his sharp metal teeth together. At least he had more than gums to meet an attack on his face.

Beyond Hellhound he saw black and transparent spirals. He realized he was in Crown's Hole. Evidently the last jab in his back had been the injection of a drug.

But Crown had not taken away his eye jewelry, nor noted his teeth. He had thought of Spar as old Eyeless Toothless.

Between Hellhound and the spirals, he saw Doc lashed to a shroud and his big black bag clipped next to him. Doc was gagged. Evidently he had tried to cry out. Spar decided not to. Doc's grey eyes were open and Spar thought Doc was looking at him.

Very slowly Spar moved his numb fingers on top of the knot lashing his wrists to the shroud and slowly contracted all his muscles and pulled. The knot slid down the shroud a millimeter. So long as he did something slowly enough, Hellhound could not see it. He repeated this action at intervals.

198

Even more slowly he swung his face to the left. He saw nothing more than that the hatch to the corridor was zipped shut, and that beyond the dog and Doc, between the black spirals, was an empty and unfurnished cabin whose whole starboard side was stars. The hatch to that cabin was open, with its black-striped emergency hatch wavering beside it.

With equal slowness he swung his face to the right, past Doc and past Hellhound, who was eagerly watching him for signs of life or waking. He had pulled down the knot on his wrists two centimeters.

The first thing he saw was a transparent oblong. In it were more stars and, by its aft edge, the smoky orange round. At last he could see more clearly. The smoke was on top, the orange underneath and irregularly placed. The whole was about as big as Spar's palm could have covered, if he had been able to stretch out his arm to full length. As he watched, he saw a bright flash in one of the orange areas. The flash was short, then it turned to a tiny black round pushing out through the smoke. More than ever, Spar felt sadness.

Below the transparency, Spar saw a horrible tableau. Suzy was strapped to a bright metal rack guyed by shrouds. She was very pale and her eyes were closed. From the side of her neck, went a red sipping-tube which forked into five branches. Four of the branches went into the red mouths of Crown, Rixende, Phanette, and Doucette. The fifth was shut by a small metal clip, and beyond it Almodie floated cowering, hands over her eyes.

Crown said softly, "We want it all. Strip her, Rixie."

Rixende clipped shut the end of her tube and swam to Suzy. Spar expected her to remove the blue culottes and bra, but instead she simply began to massage one of Suzy's legs, pressing always from ankle towards waist, driving her remaining blood nearer her neck.

Crown removed his sipping tube from his lips long enough to say, "Ahhh, good to the last drop." Then he had mouthed the blood that spurted out in the interval and had the tube in place again.

Phanette and Doucette convulsed with soundless giggles.

Almodie peered between her parted fingers, out of her mass of platinum hair, then scissored them shut again.

After a while Crown said, "That's all we'll get. Phan and Doucie, feed her to the big chewer. If you meet anyone in the passageway, pretend she's drunk. Afterwards we'll get Doc to dose us high, and give him a little brew if he behaves, then we'll drink Spar."

Spar had his wrist knot more than halfway to his teeth. Hellhound kept watching eagerly for movement, unable to see movement that slow. Slaver made tiny grey globules beside his fangs.

Phanette and Doucette opened the hatch and steered Suzy's dead body through it.

Embracing Rixende, Crown said expansively towards Doc, "Well, isn't it the right thing, old man? Nature bloody in tooth and claw, a wise one said. They've poisoned everything there." He pointed towards the smoky orange round sliding out of sight. "They're still fighting, but they'll soon all be dead. So death should be the rule too for this gimcrack, so-called survival ship. Remember they are aboard her. When we've drunk the blood of everyone aboard Windrush, including their blood, we'll drink our own, if our own isn't theirs."

Spar thought, Crown thinks too much in they's. The knot was close to his teeth. He heard the big chewer start to grind.

In the empty next cabin, Spar saw Drake and Fenner, clad once more as brewos, swimming towards the open hatch.

200

But Crown saw them too. "Get 'em, Hellhound," he directed, pointing. "It's our command."

The big black dog bulleted from his shroud through the open hatch. Drake pointed something at him. The dog went limp.

Chuckling softly, Crown took by one tip a swastika with curved, gleaming, razor-sharp blades and sent it off spinning. It curved past Spar and Doc, went through the open hatch, missed Drake and Fenner—and Hellhound—and struck the wall of stars.

There was a rush of wind, then the emergency hatch smacked shut. Spar saw Drake, Fenner, and Hellhound, wavery through the tranparent pliofilm, spew blood, bloat, burst bloodily open. The empty cabin they had been in disappeared. Windrush had a new wall and Crown's Hole was distorted.

Far beyond, growing ever tinier, the swastika spun towards the stars.

Phanette and Doucette came back. "We fed in Suzy. Someone was coming, so we beat it." The big chewer stopped grinding.

Spar bit cleanly through his wrist lashings and immediately doubled over to bite his ankles loose.

Crown dived at him. Pausing to draw knives, the four girls did the same.

Phanette, Doucette, and Rixende went limp. Spar had the impression that small black balls had glanced from their skulls.

There wasn't time to bite his feet loose, so he straightened. Crown hit his chest as Almodie hit his feet.

Crown and Spar giant-swung around the shroud. Then Almodie had cut Spar's ankles loose. As they spun off along the tangent, Spar tried to knee Crown in the groin, but Crown twisted and evaded the blow as they moved towards the inboard wall.

There was the *snick* of Crown's knife unfolding. Spar saw the dark wrist and grabbed it. He butted at Crown's jaw. Crown evaded. Spar set his teeth in Crown's neck and bit.

Blood covered Spar's face, spurted over it. He spat out a hunk of flesh. Crown convulsed. Spar fought off the knife. Crown went limp. That the pressure in a man should work against him.

Spar shook the blood from his face. Through its beads, he saw Keeper and Kim side by side. Almodie was clutching his ankles. Phanette, Doucette, Rixende floated.

Keeper said proudly, "I shot them with my gun for drunks. I knocked them out. Now I'll cut their throats, if you wish."

Spar said, "No more throat-cutting. No more blood." Shaking off Almodie's hands he took off for Doc, picking up Doucette's floating knife by the way.

He slashed Doc's lashings and cut the gag from his face.

Meanwhile Kim hissed, "Sstole and ssecreted Keeper's sscrip from the boxx. Ashshured him you sstole it, Sspar. You and SSuzzy. Sso he came. Keeper izz a shshlemiel."

Keeper said, "I saw Suzy's foot going into the big chewer. I knew it by its anklet of hearts. After that I had the courage to kill Crown or anyone. I loved Suzy."

Doc cleared his throat and croaked, "Moonmist." Spar found a triple pouch and Doc sucked it all. Doc said, "Crown spoke the truth. Windrush is a plastic survival ship from Earth. Earth—" He motioned towards the dull orange round disappearing aft in the window "—poisoned herself with smog pollution and with nuclear war. She spent gold for war, plastic for survival. Best forgotten. Windrush went mad. Understandably. Even without the Lethean ricksettia, or Styx ricks, as you call it. Thought Windrush was the cosmos. Crown kidnapped me to get my drugs, kept me alive to know the doses."

Spar looked at Keeper. "Clean up here," he ordered. "Feed Crown to the big chewer."

Almodie pulled herself from Spar's ankles to his waist. "There was a second survival ship. Circumluna. When Windrush went mad, my father and mother—and you—were sent here, to investigate and cure. But my father died and you got Styx ricks. My mother died just before I was given to Crown. She sent you Kim."

Kim hissed, "My fforebear came from Circumluna to Windrush, too. Great grandmother. Taught me ffigures for Windrushsh . . . Radiuss from moon-ccenter, 2,500 miles. Period, ssixx hours—sso, the sshort dayss. A terranth izz the time it takess Earth to move through a consstellation, and sso on."

Doc said, "So Spar, you're the only one who remembers without cynicism. You'll have to take over. It's all yours, Spar."

Spar had to agree.

CAT
POEMS

CONTRIBUTORS

MARGO SKINNER
KAREN ANDERSON
POUL ANDERSON

EARTH BOUND

Turned to a commonplace and every man's dream
(Or for his sons),
The race in silver ships for the starstream
Is now the stuff for scientists, cadets, and big guns,
Astrostrategists who would make a bomb bay of the Moon
And martial politicians arming Mars.

We were the pioneers from distant stars.
Our home was Altair; we, the eagle-born,
Moved in our Pinta through a thousand galaxies,
Making our charts, and marking "Here be dragons,"
Here night flowers that drink pure selenium,
Here the stone people, speaking the Old Language.

Oh, our world was fair,
Resplendent under the blazing orb of Altair;
Yet our spirits craved more:
The rainbow waves of the distant shore,
Oceans of opals and shores of pearl.

Our Companion understood our hearts.
His green eyes flamed; he was ever a far-ranger.
If we had left him, he would not have died,
But turned to the turquoise jungles, away from men,
And forgotten our language, become wild again.

207

So he traveled with us, delighting in free fall,
Dancing in space, attacking a flower ball,
Talking to us in the long night
When we wearied of free flight
And even of each other.

So it came to this:
This green world dying in its own smoke.
Our ship broken and memories blasted,
We move among these rigid streets, trees bound in stone.
Here we are alone: even from each other.

Only in dreams do we remember
Lost voyages and the fragrance of far stars,
And in each other's eyes, a moment only.

The Companion purrs, forgetful by the fire.
Yet sometimes his green eyes flash into flame.
Almost he calls you by the old name
And remembers when he played among the stars.

—Margo Skinner

GOD AND THE CAT

God carries a cat
In the curve of His arm.
Purring it looks at Him,
Full in the eyes.
Green eyes are fearless.
Claws knead His arm.

"Courageous, destructible, impudent creature!"
God smiles
And strokes soft fur
With His great hand.

—Margo Skinner

A SINISTER OF SIAMESE

Had a cat named Tomien.
In the dead of night she played Chopin.

Had a cat named Little Blue.
Mated him with a cat named Green.
All of the kittens were aquamarine.

Had a cat named Fatima.
She would pat you with her paw.

Had a wild cat named Kim.
Couldn't do a thing with him.

Had a cat named O-Ho-San.
She drank tea as if in Japan.

Had an elegant cat named Jade
Who would thrust black velvet nose
Into the petals of the rose.

Had a mad cat named Kwan Yew.
He stole mittens
And little kittens.
He loved 'em too.

—Margo Skinner

211

LULLABY FOR A CAT NAMED FATIMA

Sleepy-byo,
Kitty pie-o,
Kitty pie-o,
Sleepy-byo.

Close your blue eyes,
Curl your fur up,
Head on forepaws,
Whiskers twitching,
Pink tongue peeping,
Sleeping, sleeping.

Dreaming your cat dreams,
Growl a little,
Chasing monsters;
Purr a little,
Washing kittens;
Stir a little,
Sniffing spring wind.

Sleeping softly,
Royally dreaming
Of the olden time
In Egyptian clime
When you were Bast, a queen.

Sleepy-byo,
Kitty pie-o,
Kitty pie-o,
Sleepy-byo.

—Margo Skinner

ORIGIN OF THE SPECIES

I can see it now: they were ready to lift gravs
(Or whatever they did) but the cats weren't in the ship.
"Here, kitty!" they called, in whatever outlandish way
They spoke to cats; but the cats were out in the sun
Rolling about and sparring, and didn't come.
They held the airlock open, with tentacles
Or claws or something, that clenched impatiently
(I know how they felt) but the cats still wouldn't come.
And then they tried to catch them; well, what good
Has that ever done, when cats don't feel like coming?
The cats scampered off, flicking their tails in the air,
And all climbed up in some trees; and there they sat
Sneeringly patient. Nothing could be done—
It was time to leave—they put it in the log,
"Third planet of Athfan's Star: the cats deserted."

——Karen Anderson

215

SESTINA OF THE CAT IN THE DOORWAY

At my command, he's opened up the door;
its jaws distend across a gape of night
and winds give words, not in the tongue of man
nor dealing with a hearthfire or with cream,
out of those wooden lips to call a cat
toward ancient roads—or so, at least, I think.

Moon-ghostly wind-words give a cat to think
while standing in their mumble at the door:
the wind's akin to all the tribe of cat,
who still remember how another night
was filled with saber teeth and blood—no cream
to trap the tiger in the cave of man!

The bird called Fear within the ribs of man
must flutter crippled wings when humans think
that all the world's not cushions, light, and cream,
but turns at last to darkness, when the door
alone stands guard against the flowing night
and prowling wind and hunger of the cat.

It's plain to see in twilight how the cat
exists to be appeased by blinded man,
for most of this tall cosmos is a night,
and men must squeak like fieldmice when they think
of hungry stars that hunt beyond their door;
therefore they bribe the child of night with cream.

POUL ANDERSON

And yet, bleak dignity is not the cream
which bought the thunder querning in the cat,
and truth to tell, there's pleasure in a door,
the wooden carapace of clawless man,
and fire is fragrant when you pause to think
of gaunt, black, windy, and owl-haunted night.

Indeed, the wish to be of tiger night
and lap the blood of birds in place of cream:
to flow, another shadow, and to think
on glacier years when mammoth and when cat
cried whetted fear into the guts of man—
is tattered by the wind within the door.

Unrestful night wakes rovings in a cat,
but hearth and cream and cushions speak for man.
I'll have to think. Don't shut that goddam door!

———Poul Anderson

AFTERWORD
MARGO SKINNER

Afterword

Fritz's newest book is an anthology of his unique cat fantasies, based largely on felines he has known and some we have shared in common.

Gummitch is well-loved by Leiber cat fans; Psycho is a charmer; and the others who share billing with him are interesting in their own right.

It is in "Cat Three" that Fritz introduces us to some of the "Sinister of Siamese" of my poem. Originally I met them when I lived in a quasi-commune in San Francisco, whose tenants included a smashing French-Canadian young woman, now a professor in Montreal, a dizzy young American blonde, a male member of the original Jefferson Airplane, and various others, who came and went. Lois, the mistress of the large flat we shared, had been a bohemian since her youth, originally in Greenwich Village, a leftist activist, a San Francisco beatnik, and, when I knew her, a hippie. In the flat she raised pedigreed sealpoint Siamese cats, quite illegally. At one time there were seventeen adults and kittens. The two to whom I was closest were Fatima, a sweet matron, and Kim, her child, a wild little fellow, whose teeth marks are still on my arms. Not that he was vicious: he just didn't want me to go to work and leave him.

Kim's father, incidentally, was the brightest cat I ever knew. Among his achievements, he not only used the people toilet, but neatly pulled the plunger after himself.

Eventually, I inherited both Fatima and Kim, who first show up in Fritz's fiction as Cleopatra and Caesar in "Cat Three." Miss Skipsy is sort of based on Margo. Marc Antony, the third cat in the story, is an imaginative creation, who in some respects resembles Fritz.

Kim turns up again in "The Bump," where his habits of throwing clothes out of dresser drawers and "bulging under the blanket" of my bed, are very recognizable. Fatima again appears as his mother.

They are present once more in "The Great San Francisco Glacier," as is this writer. I think Fritz got the original idea from my seldom-defrosted Frigidare.

Fatima lived a healthy twenty-three years and then suddenly, almost literally, crumpled up. Kim lived to be ten, then, greatly stressed, both by the death of his mother and our removal to another house, suddenly died. They are both buried in Bubbling Wells, a pet cemetery in the Napa Hills with a spendid view of the Bay and San Francisco beyond, where another delightful cat, the beautiful Sarah, a loving Himalayan, has joined them. For each we had a wake, with Fritz doing the obsequies followed by drinks and good Italian dinner with friends, including some pet cemetery staff.

My own idea is to join those kitties there when the time comes. All of us, temporarily resurrected, will dance on the hills and look down at the lights of the City.

Dear readers, Fritz and I were married on May 15, 1992, and had a smashing wedding reception on the 17th. Our current cats, Lulu, a sweet tortoiseshell of thirteen, and Mr. Mouser, a big handsome white cat with light green eyes, helped receive. Mouser came with that name. We wish all our friends could have attended. Love long and prosper.

Margo Skinner
(Mrs. Fritz Leiber)

FRITZ LEIBER TRIBUTES

FRITZ'S INTRODUCTION TO
GUMMITCH AND FRIENDS

GUMMITCH AND FRIENDS

This illustrated first edition is limited
to 1,000 copies for sale.

This is copy _____

FRITZ LEIBER

Margo Skinner Leiber

MARGO SKINNER

Roger Gerberding

ROGER GERBERDING

FRITZ LEIBER

1910 - 1992

Fritz, Jonquil, and Friend

PREFACE

Last Fall as the World Fantasy Convention was coming to a close and the lobby of our Tucson hotel was churning with farewells, Fritz quietly handed me a copy of Margo's *As Green as Emeraude.* Inside, his inscription read "Looking forward to the job with Roger G." Nothing more needed to be said. I smiled all the way back to New Hampshire, opening the little book to reread those few words several times midflight. So began *Gummitch and Friends.*

During the winter months that followed my mind frequently wandered back to Tucson where it's warm, and lemons—not icicles—hang within arms-reach. At Christmastime in San Francisco, Fritz and Margo hung a small clay ornament, a memento of Arizona, on their tree and celebrated with a gathering on Post Street. We spoke often by phone. As stories were gathered and illustrations prepared, Fritz worked on "Thrice the Brinded Cat"—his first fictional piece in more than two years. Our project was progressing with energy and enthusiasm. The endpaper illustrations went to press only days before Margo discovered that she had cancer. Good news followed bad when, after more than two decades together, Fritz and Margo "impetuously" (to borrow a word from Herb Caen's column describing the event) were married at City Hall.

I suppose they were still on their honeymoon when I stayed with them on Post Street. Lulu and Mister Mouser, resident feline companions, shared my room. Fritz was bright and quietly charming and Margo, who was about to begin chemotherapy, remarkably cheerful. I remember returning to the apartment one evening in time for "Jeopardy," a nightly favorite there. Fritz never missed a question. From ancient history to Rock & Roll, he had all the answers and in a lively, animated half-hour variously cheered and chastised his fellow contestants. He'd have been the all-time champ. When I left, he rode down with me on the temperamental elevator and stood curbside. He was tall and elegant and gentlemanly. It was the last time I saw Fritz.

In late Summer, Fritz and Margo left San Francisco for Toronto where Fritz was to be a guest of honor at RhinoCon. Margo, who was undergoing chemotherapy, had the go-ahead from her doctors. It was during that trip that Fritz suffered several small strokes from which he never recovered.

During the last days of his life, as Fritz lay in hospital in San Francisco, he asked Margo to bring the endpapers for this deluxe edition of *Gummitch and Friends* so that he could sign them. He simply did not have the strength to do so.

In September, at the World Science Fiction Convention in Orlando, Florida, we received a phone call from Margo announcing Fritz's death.

Knowing how important *Gummitch and Friends* was to Fritz, Margo asked that we go forward with the deluxe edition, leaving the signature pages in place. At her request, a special chapter was added to this volume—a tribute to Fritz Leiber.

We thank Justin Leiber, Poul Anderson, Karen Anderson, Robert Bloch, Ray Bradbury, Ramsey Campbell, Catherine Crook de Camp, L. Sprague de Camp, Harlan Ellison, Dennis Etchison, Stephen King, Judith Merril, Andre Norton, and Frank M. Robinson for their contributions to this deluxe edition. And we thank Fritz for giving all of us so much pleasure for so many years.

—Ann R. Howland
Donald M. Grant, Publisher, Inc
October, 1992

Fritz Leiber, Felines and Son

by Justin Leiber

Gummitch was a real cat, of course. I saw the dilapidated little guy a couple of hours after Fritz had rescued him, the only one living from a litter abandoned in a backyard thicket in a snowy, bitterly cold Chicago. Fritz, wearing a light brown, terry cloth bathrobe, was feeding him warmed milk with an eyedropper. Gummitch lost half his tail to frost bite and his roughish looking face and expression seemed to me, as he grew to be a tom cat, a result of his early exposure. I didn't see much of Fritz, my mother Jonquil, and Gummitch after they moved to Los Angeles for the 1960s, though we corresponded frequently, naturally exchanging photographs of our cat friends, and I savored with delight the ever varied and ever fascinating appearances of felines in Fritz's fiction.

Indeed I suspect that no human writer has ever accorded felines as much respect and attention. Quite apart from these charming accounts of Gummitch's (and versions of Fritz and Jonquil's) doings, we have, among many examples, the peace-making, extraterrestrial green feline, Lucky, of Fritz's *Green Millennium,* a rollicking cold war sendup that had the unique distinction of simultaneous condemnation by the *Wall Street Journal* and *Pravda.* And who could forget Tiger-ishka, the arrogant, human-sized feline alien of *The Wanderer?*

Doubtless, the felines reciprocated Fritz's love and respect in their own cattish way. How else to explain the strange series of events that brought Fritz and me closer together through the 1980s? This real life story is worth telling, if only because of the delight it afforded him.

After my wife moved out and I lost my tenure at the City University of New York in the budgetary crunch of 1976, I ended up (courtesy, Noam Chomsky) with the breathing space of a temporary visiting scientist position at MIT, which gave me a respectable address, a desk, a subsidized apartment, and little else of my old life except my unemployment checks and two blue point siamese, Charles and Mizmo, who were undoubtedly the local agents of felinity incorporated. At loose ends, I wrote "Fritz Leiber and Eyes," which was ostensibly a spell cast to get Fritz back to his writing. To quote the climax of it, which starts out appealing to cats and then goes on to his whole menagerie,

> Go, little stories, caper seductively or raucously around his bed—Go, little stories, and fling his fingers on the typewriter keys . . . Go little stories, and change the street numbers so the fans can't find him—fox the postal machines so his mail goes to Auckland, New Zealand, and viper the wires so that incoming calls move by spidery indirection from initial dialing to total confusion. Shake hailstones down large as spearmint blossoms if he dawdles in the streets or runs unnecessary errands. Sprinkle dust of Yeats and Poe, and toenail clippings of Robert Graves and Ingmar Bergman, in protective circles round his rooms. Go little stories, and pull some strings. Fritz Leiber is for the stars.

Though Fritz, and some other SF people, found the piece amusing, and Fritz did resume writing, I suspect (this is often the case with real magic) that the spell hit me more than anything else. In any case, I wrote the first pages of what was to become my first novel, *Beyond Rejection*, and Charles and Mizmo somehow arranged that I took a professorship at the University of Houston.

It wasn't until January of my first academic year at the University that I learned that the University had a real, live cougar mascot—better yet, Shasta IV, a just two year old, hundred pound female, and the retired Shasta III, a fifteen year old, arthritic female. (Cougars live about six or seven years in the wild, about nine or ten in zoos; III was a grande dame indeed, whom we accompanied on her exercise walks around campus with a little red wagon, to which she sometimes retired when she had walked enough.) I began writing Fritz long accounts of my experiences with the cougars, especially with IV, who had a little bark and a wonderful rumbling purr, and who eventually came to welcome me by doing loop-the-loops on the ceiling of her cage. The Guard eventually allowed me to join after I proved to be an addition to the circle of three whom Shasta IV would allow to put a collar and chain on her, preparatory to leaving her cage (I got several superficial gashes and two puncture wounds the one time, early in our relationship, that Shasta decided to test me.) By this time I also had written about half of *Beyond Rejection*. But it lacked something.

When Fritz told me by phone, emphatically, "Get the cat in it!" I was sure he didn't mean Charles or Mizmo. He was surely right. I came to chose the big cat sections when asked to give a reading from the novel after a fan commented on how real the interactions between my protagonist and the big cat seemed. Naturally, once I started publishing F&SF, Fritz and I started to get together a lot at conventions. We worked out one hell of a father/son cat and cougar act.

Fritz was a hippy before and long after there were hippies and a gentleman—i.e. someone who is not a wage slave—long after the word was cashiered. I put it down to the influence, the love, of cats.

—Justin Leiber

FRITZ LEIBER

BY POUL ANDERSON

"When half-Gods go
The Gods arrive."

Yes, but what do you do when the Gods themselves depart?

Ever more of late the great ones have been leaving us, the creators who in the Golden Age made science fiction and fantasy what they are to this day, and continued in their greatness until the end. Now Fritz Leiber is gone.

Memories follow him like shadows cast by his tall figure—no, not only memories, but works that endure, from such dazzling early originalities as *Conjure Wife* and *Gather, Darkness!* on through the years to his very last. He was never content to repeat himself but was always in quest of new frontiers, always delighting us not only with his style and wit but with wellspring freshness.

This, though, is not the place to discuss the writings. Literary historians will be doing that for a long time. So will his colleagues, who owe him so much, and countless enchanted readers. Here I would just like to share a few recollections of the man himself.

I first saw him at the 1949 world science fiction convention in Cincinnati. Back then, those affairs were small and friendly; you could actually meet people, relax and get a bit acquainted. Towering, classically handsome, Fritz was as impressive personally as his writings. Yet he was soft-spoken, modest, amiable, lovable. The opinion I formed of him then, I expressed long afterward when the honor became mine of doing an introduction to *The Best of Fritz Leiber:* "It is etymologically wrong but psychologically right to define a gentle-man as one who is gentle, yet very much a man." I went on to say something about his having been at various times a championship fencer, a chess player rated expert, an actor, a lay preacher, a drama instructor, a staff writer for different publications, and much else. "And, of course," I observed, "in his writing he has stared down—or laughed down—death, horror, human absurdity, with guts worthy of a Jeffers, Kafka, or Cervantes."

However, this is not the place for a biography, either. He wrote about himself with rare candor and objectivity, while in a number of his stories there is a strong autobiographical element. If the academic establishment ever notices, it will find it has on its hands another Montaigne, Pepys, or Boswell.

We didn't have much more contact until the mid-fifties, when he and his wife Jonquil moved to southern California from the Midwest. They visited my wife Karen and me in our home, and we visited them in theirs, from time to time, and we'd also meet now and then at conventions or parties. The occasions were always grand for the Andersons, who hope the Leibers enjoyed them too. It's not betraying any secrets to admit that Fritz and Jonquil had something of an alcohol problem. But it never lessened his courtesy and, what's deeper, his graciousness. Rather, sometimes when he'd had a few he'd recite G.K. Chesterton's flamboyant ballad "Lepanto" in that wonderful stage voice, and wasn't hearing this an experience!

Eventually Jonquil's health failed. I've heard that some women were talking about it among themselves, and one said, "Yes, I hope she gets well, but if she goes, then I want him." To which another replied, "Oh, no, you don't. You'll take your place in line with the rest of us."

Jonquil died. Fritz's elegy to her, in a booklet of his poems, is among the most touching things I have ever read. He moved to San Francisco, overcame his alcoholism, and burst into a nova-like brilliance in writing that never afterward faded.

Nor did his lively interest in everything around him. He

grew intimate with his adopted city, discovering many things that most natives never suspected were there. Readers of *Locus* saw his regular column, in which he discussed not only his hobby of astronomy but practically any other subject. Even at the last, as physical infirmities closed in, he was going to conventions and being one of their liveliest attenders. Meanwhile he became a great-grandfather and his long-time close friend Margo Skinner became his second wife. Surely all our hearts now go out to her.

In my introduction I told how on 13 July 1973 Karen "gave an elaborate dinner to honor the memory of E.R. Eddison, upon the date of Lessingham's translation into Zimiamvia. Only those who would understand what that means were invited, and they were expected to come in costume. Fritz graced the party as the oldest, most sharply humorous, and best-dressed man present." What I will now add is that, as he and I sat on the lawn of this suburban house, waiting for the food to be ready, a hummingbird came a-hover and we watched it for a while. He remarked that it's all wrong that those creatures are New World; something so exquisite ought to be Japanese. The thought lives on in me because of being so very Fritz Leiber.

—Poul Anderson

BALLADE OF A LOSS

FRITZ LEIBER: 1910-1992

BY KAREN ANDERSON

Where's Gummitch, sprung from time and space,
And Armon Jarles whose beliefs were crime?
Where Snakes and Spiders, who retrace
And re-split all the forks of time
By stabbing in an alley's slime
Or skies ablaze with weaponthroe?
The Smoke Ghost made of urban grime?
Ah, but where is last year's snow?

Where's Tigerishka, wandering dame,
Or Paul, the ape she lulled with rhyme?
Zane Gort, of robot-adventure fame?
Or Thorn, whose destiny was trine?
Where's Tansy Saylor, with no dime
Of silver to set against her foe,
The Hempnell wives who laid conjure-lime?
Ah, but where is last year's snow?

Four Ghosts in Hamlet—who can say?
The Cleveland Depths, mad Niflheim?
Sheelba, Ningauble, where are they,
And all the folk of Lankhmar's clime?
Where's Fafhrd, mighty in his prime,
And where did subtle Mouser go,
Who faced the gods on the Isle of Rime?
Ah, but where is last year's snow?

Envoi
Fritz, you were like a peak sublime
Amid a great sierra's show
That now is dry of the brooklets' chime;
Ah, but where is last year's snow?

                              —Karen Anderson

Fritz Leiber

by Robert Bloch

There are those of us who love cats and those of us who love dogs some love both, others detest all animals. Thus it's difficult to generalize correctly about pets or the people who prefer them.

But in some cases it's possible to particularize. And with Fritz Leiber there's no problem at all.

Fritz Loved cats.

He relished the commonality of their calm, shared their silent serenity. Dog-lovers are different: they want more bark for their buck. A canine-fancier tends to enjoy an atmosphere of noisy over-excitement, overreaction and all-round emotional excess.

While it is true that cats are prone to complain loudly when they're in heat (don't we all?), their usual demeanor is one of quiet dignity and reserve, very much like that of Fritz himself.

Fritz was a child of the theater, no stranger to professional appearances before paying audiences when he toured in his father's repertory company. He had a commanding stature, a striking appearance and a trained, mellifluous voice, but there was a significant difference between the young actor and the mature man who moved offstage into the writing world. Fritz Leiber, despite his thespic talents, was never "on"—his private *persona* was not that of a performer.

Those who saw him for the first time at a science fiction convention or social gathering might well be inclined to note his presence, for his height alone made him outstanding. But his voice never rose above conversational level in a crowd or at a dining-table; he didn't call attention to himself with jest or gesticulation. His was a modest and unobtrusive presence.

It seems to work well for cats, but it may have hindered Fritz in his chosen calling. Over the years, as writers ceased to be isolationists and were forced into the self-promotion of newspaper, magazine, radio and television interviews, bookstore appearances, seminars and symposia, the tendency on their part has been to become louder and funnier—or, at least, louder.

Not Fritz. An accomplished speaker and reciter of his own and other authors' works, he retained restraint. He was, as they used to say, one cool cat. Perhaps for this reason he never rose from midlist to bestseller celebrity, though colleagues all knew, respected (and sometimes envied) his brilliant talent.

There was sadness in his life, and much misfortune. But through it all the grave and gentle grace of the man lent an air of feline felicity to his deportment, plus a hint of a cat's complexity—the laidback manner masking inner tensions. One senses this combination in various aspects of the work as well as the man, and it forms part of the appeal inherent in both.

The man is gone now but his work remains. And this present volume offers ample evidence of why it will endure.

Even the dog-fanciers will appreciate it. You don't have to love cats to love Leiber.

—Robert Bloch

FRITZ LEIBER

BY RAY BRADBURY

There are several reasons for me to write this piece: Fritz Leiber and the cats, or, more properly for cat lovers, Cats and Fritz Leiber. As the one-time owner of 22 cats, count 'em, 22! I am tempted to place Fritz below the cats, but there is no way to do that. Memories prevent.

The first memory has to do with the summer of 1947 when I was in my mid-twenties and Fritz, some years ahead of me, came to visit me in Venice, California where I lived because I was poor. My income, if and when it came in, was roughly twenty to thirty dollars a week, selling short stories to *Weird Tales, Amazing Stories, Thrilling Wonder* and *Dime Detective* for one or two cents a word. My first book of stories had just been published and was selling at the incredible rate of twenty copies a week cross-country, so when Fritz arrived it was like royalty visiting the chicken ranch.

In my parent's front room (I was still living at home; couldn't afford to move out into the world) he inscribed his book of stories to me, as follows: "I am sitting in Ray's parlor looking out at Ray's 'Night'." I had, you see, already claimed the Night as my country and even though his book was titled *Night's Black Agents*, he generously handed over the darkest part of the territory to me. The evening flowed on, not as mentor to student, which indeed it was to me, but as friend to friend.

Two years later, with little money in the bank, and my wife Maggie pregnant with our first child, I traveled by Greyhound Bus to New York, hoping to sell some of my stories to the publishers there. I placed *The Martian Chronicles* with Doubleday for the amazing down payment of $750.00 and stopped over in Chicago on my way home, where Fritz and his wife,

Jonquil, gave me a bed for the night and wondrous conversation until three a.m. Again, though I did not say so, I felt I was the ukulele player in the presence of the master of the cello, who welcomed me with warmth, intelligence, and humanity.

Those were the days, of course, long before the Space Age, when we writers of science or science-fantasy fiction needed each other much like those medieval monks who half hid from the world and guarded their night-candled libraries. The critics and the schools had yet to discover what seemed to us obvious merits in prophecy and imagination.

So it was that one of Fritz's best works, *Gather Darkness*, was published by Pellegrini & Codahy in 1950. I considered it then, and I consider it now, a work that deserves to be fleshed out and dramatized on the screen. On numerous occasions I have bought copies of the novel and handed them to producers and directors hoping they had enough imagination to focus its energy on the screen. But then, and perhaps even now, those directors I approached were fearful of reactions from The Church, though I never quite believed such repercussions would follow the release of what might have been a truly insightful and refreshing film. Its central idea of future scientists using technology to control the masses remains fresh and vital today.

All of which brings me to my final point. The future of Fritz Leiber still lies ahead. I am willing to predict the filming of a number of his works. But I steadfastly believe that *Gather Darkness*, in good time, with the proper director, will find its place in cinema history. At its premiere, I hope to attend as interlocutor, usher, ticket-taker and first-class publicity man. It *will* be done. Who says? *I* say.

—Ray Bradbury
Los Angeles,
October 7, 1992